CONEJO VALLEY WRITERS: WRITERS HELPING WRITERS

An Anthology

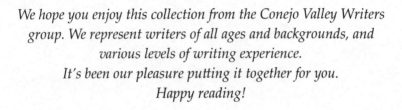

We hope you enjoy this collection from the Conejo Valley Writers group. We represent writers of all ages and backgrounds, and various levels of writing experience.
It's been our pleasure putting it together for you.
Happy reading!

CONTENTS

FLASH FICTION-- 9

Deborah Brawders: LURED ------------------------------------11

Bob Calverley: A TALE OF TWO COCKERS----------------16

Gabriel Fergesen: TALES OF ATLANTIS SIX----------------21

Mark Frankcom: ROBOTS --------------------------------------34

Alex Holub: WHAT WAS THAT? ------------------------------36

Hal T. Horowitz: STATE ROUTE 733--------------------------39

Jeanne Rawlings: LIGHT WITHOUT FLAMES ------------48

J. Schubert: GOING TO POT ------------------------------------54

Theresa Schultz: THE ROCK------------------------------------56

Marcia Smart: THE THANKSGIVING VISIT ----------------59

Alan Richard Zimmerman: DEATH--------------------------64

Deborah Brawders: RETURN TO SENDER -----------------71

Alex Holub: APRIL FOOLS--------------------------------------75

Hal T. Horowitz: ELDERS OF BAYVIEW --------------------82

Jeanne Rawlings: THE THOUSAND STEPS ----------------91

THE GIFT OF POETRY --97

Barbara Champlin: UNTITLED --------------------------------99

Barbara Champlin: SUPREME COURT BLUES ---------- 101

Jamie Diep: A TRIBUTE TO LOVE ------------------------- 103

Jamie Diep: WHAT IS LIFE?----------------------------------- 105

Michael Edelstein: SONNETS FOR MY BELOVED A -- 107

Michael Edelstein: SONNETS FOR MY BELOVED B -- 108

Bonnie Goldenberg: APPROACHING 80 ----------------- 110

Claudine Mason-Marx: THE CRESCENT AND THE
    THISTLE -- 114

Tamara Nowlin: ABYSS--- 116

Tamara Nowlin: JANUARY ----------------------------------- 117

Tamara Nowlin: SEEN --- 118

Alan Richard Zimmerman: WINTER ---------------------- 120

LOOKING BACK IN TIME ------------------------------------ 123

Bob Calverley: THE WORST DAY OF MY LIFE---------- 125

Michael Edelstein: ONCE A KID FROM BROOKLYN - 131

Mark Frankcom: WAKING UP ------------------------------ 137

Claudine Mason-Marx: LILAC SKY------------------------ 140

Stephen Marks: TEN-YEAR JOURNEY TO
    "AUTHORDOM" --- 142

Judy Panczak: AUGIE -- 148

Kathleen Galloway Rogan: PAPER DOLLS---------------- 155

Marcia Smart: DIARY OF A WIMPY CAMPER ---------- 159

J. Schubert: THIRTEEN HOURS IN A DIFFERENT
    WORLD --- 164

Judy Watson: MILLIE THE GOLDFISH -------------------- 169

Judy Watson: RECOLLECTIONS OF LEE BREUER ----- 176

The History of the Conejo Valley Writers --------------------183

Acknowledgments ---185

FLASH FICTION

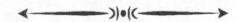

LURED

Deborah Brawders

It's getting closer, raging like an angry poltergeist intent on harm. Never traveling alone, it has a deadlier partner who will creep under the door, invading the space where I am captive.

I feel a trickle of sweat running down my lip, which mixes with the tardy tears of contrition.

It's too late to do any good now.

I see my alarm clock in the haze, green numbers counting down the minutes. It was all part of your grand design that I should sit and contemplate my end.

That impatient intruder is at my bedroom door. It has come for me. I want it over quickly, yet part of me believes I will escape. I clench my fists and strain at the rope that binds me to the chair.

I fell into your trap.

I should have been more cautious. It's easy to say, now that I have my eyes pressed against the crystal clear lens of hindsight.

I chose a rendezvous on a bright afternoon in a very public place. I thought I was so careful, but you found a way around all my precautions.

Now I realize the bio on the dating website was fake. The shadowy figure in the emails didn't exist. A prepaid credit card covered all the expenses of the dating site, with no trail back to you. You laid a series of clever clues, luring me into your trap. You used my profile to create the perfect persona. All those carefully chosen words seduced my eager heart. Even the name Trailblazer was a devilishly clever play on words. The grainy photograph gave you just enough good looks and lean figure to please the eye.

Then came an offer to meet.

A year ago, I would never have agreed to meet a masked stranger on a blind date. COVID changed the landscape on which we conducted our lives, and you took full advantage.

I couldn't resist.

My date would be wearing a black mask and carrying a yellow carnation. I glowed with anticipation now that the perfect soulmate was within reach.

Embarrassingly early, I killed time, wandering through a sea of COVID masks. I spotted the seated figure with a splash of bright yellow. I knew you had been watching me from behind those dark glasses, shrouded in that hat and mask.

I wasn't alarmed.

I should have been.

The virus provided the perfect camouflage. It left me staring at my faceless companion, leaving my imagination to fill in all the blanks from your photo. I graciously accepted the coffee that you had waiting for me. If I had stopped rambling, I would have realized I gave away everything and learned nothing of you. My perfect date had a soft voice with a calming lilt. A slight accent I couldn't peg for north or south. All your words were like a warm blanket, designed to enchant me. Naturally, I fell for a character skewed to meet my every expectation.

I stepped into your web.

Your gloved hand reached over and touched me. My quizzical glance brought forth your strange answer. "You can't be too careful. After all, the ides of March are upon us."

I missed the warning.

I removed my mask to drink, hoping yours might drop away too.

It didn't.

We parted as the late afternoon sun dipped below the horizon. Deliriously happy, I took no precautions.

We had a second date for lunch.

Lunch is so safe.

I rushed home.

You followed me and slipped through the side door that I foolishly left unlocked. You appeared in my bedroom doorway, dark and menacing. Instead of the carnation, a yellow cord dangled from your gloved hand.

I'm at the mercy of all your sinister intentions.

I try to stand, but a leaden feeling creeps through my veins.

Reality hits. You had laced my coffee. Now I am all yours.

You finally drop the mask that hid your ravaged face. The burned flesh has a molten quality, and in your eyes I see vestiges of pain. The dissolved skin gives your lopsided grin a sinister cast. Your gloves come off, revealing scarred hands. Clawlike, they reach up and remove the hat and wig, revealing hair matted in sparse clumps.

Then it comes to me: "Beware the Ides of March." Shakespeare, of course, and I recall it has a more ominous meaning. March is the Roman deadline for settling debts. The day they murdered Julius Caesar. All the subtle hints flood my consciousness. Best of all was the yellow carnation. I remember now it is the flower of contempt and disdain.

I understand it all too late.

The internet was the fertile hunting ground that led Trailblazer right to my door. I happily littered social media with intimate details of my past, present, and future.

I was easy prey.

Why the subterfuge?

Why not just come and get me?

My desperate pleas fall unheard against those cold, melted ears. I can tell from your flint-colored eyes that nothing would save me.

A chance encounter long ago. You, a lone hitchhiker, and I, the Good Samaritan. I didn't mean for it to happen, that accident on a lonely country lane. I had been drinking. I left the scene. I told the police someone stole my car. It gave me an out, with few questions from my insurance company. Later I learned the car caught fire, with the passenger I had left to face all my consequences trapped inside. I still kept silent.

As your inferno races towards me, I reflect on the fire in my car. I see you in the small metal box, your flesh melting into those plastic seats, the seat belt buckle blazing hot and the door handle almost gone. I'm sure you were thinking of the gas tank behind you. How much time did you have?

I can taste your terror rising in my throat. I'll be dead before it reaches me. At least, I hope so. I already smell the acrid tang of smoke whose wispy fingers curl toward me, caressing my face like a deadly lover.

As I wait for the end, I have time to admonish myself. I wish I could cut off all the sharp edges of my life and file them smooth to the touch. If only I could rewrite the past.

I met the invisible being. Someone cloaked in a hat, mask, and glasses. The police will never catch Trailblazer; COVID made sure of that.

You played fair and led me down a path strewn with warnings.

I threw you no such lifeline.

The burning air teases my skin. There will be no emergency call from a neighbor for, like the quiet country lane where I left you, my house is also far from the madding crowd. Everyone will say I gave Trailblazer a life sentence in that ruined face.

Tit for tat.

She came to claim her pound of flesh.

Deborah Brawders, a.k.a. Katie Crow, was born in London and has lived in Africa, the Middle East, and California. In her books, written under the nom de plume of Katie Crow, she draws on these nomadic wanderings to create a cast of unusual characters and set them in places with dark, intriguing histories. Most days you can find Deborah hiking, gardening, or running plot ideas past her trusty companion, a rescued terrier named Winston.

To learn more about Deborah's books, visit her author website at: https://katiecrow.com/

A TALE OF TWO COCKERS

Bob Calverley

It's Friday night at the double-wide veterinary clinic, and I'm eating day-old Krispy Kremes for dinner. Just chased off a woman, her kid, and her scrawny cat with a middle finger salute. So what if I left the front light on? Doesn't mean I'm open.

I'm tired. Wasted most of the day with an emergency tooth extraction. Stupid, overweight cocker spaniel had a fatal anesthesia allergy. Had to console the old bag who owned the smelly beast. OK, it wasn't consoling. More like lawsuit avoidance and extracting payment for the extraction. Also, payment to incinerate Joe, the allergic cocker.

The vet school dean said I'd end up in a place like Horn City, Texas, population 1,123. Most people here are old farts living with their runny-eyed rat-dogs and Salvation Army furniture in this sad trailer park. Three days a week, I work shifts at clinics in El Paso to keep from starving. I wish old Doc Cramdon would hurry up and croak from his cancer so I can take over the lucrative hog farm trade.

The doorbell clangs. What the hell? I turned the damn light off. At the door, I find a midget with two pet carriers.

"Hello, got a couple o' emergencies here," the midget says in a gravelly voice.

"I'm not really open . . ."

"I'm Daedalus Smoot, and I can pay cash."

The magic words. "What kind of emergencies?"

There's a bark from one of the pet carriers, and I bend down to see another cocker spaniel, this one a mean-looking, slavering beast with a large head and undocked tail.

"Cerberus has been throwing up a lot," Smoot says.

Cerberus?

Potbellied and bowlegged, Smoot's dressed in lizard-skin boots, kiddie blue jeans, a sleeveless yellow leather jerkin over a pink cowboy shirt, and a giant green Stetson. Under four feet high, he looks like a Texas garden gnome. Never met him, never seen him before, but I've heard of him. Everybody in Horn City has. Owns half the town, including a big warehouse stuffed with computer servers. Richest guy in Horn City. Supposed to be an eccentric inventor.

I examine the dog without getting bitten and can't find anything wrong. "He seems fine. Probably just something he ate. What's in the other carrier?"

"Oh, um, let me show you." Smoot pulls off a faded beach towel covering the carrier. Inside is the biggest mosquito I've ever seen.

How in hell could a mosquito grow this large? The tubular abdomen is a foot and a half long, with striped yellow and black segments. Six slender legs emanate from a black thorax that's not as long as the abdomen, but far bulkier. Two veined wings attached to the thorax flap at me. The head is the size of a softball and consists mostly of massive eyes with dozens of tiny domes glittering in the clinic lights. A long, skinny organ, the proboscis, extends from the head, flanked by two skinny feelers.

I shudder. "Jesus wept. What am I supposed to do with this?"

"I made a mistake," Smoot says. He nods vigorously, making his hat go crooked. "See, I have this invention, the metampholyzer." From his back pocket, he takes out a shiny metal cylinder the size of a small flashlight. "You can exchange any animal, any living thing, actually, one into another. But I'm still working out the um . . . bugs."

We stare at each other.

"Anyway, I accidentally exchanged my daughter with a mosquito," he says. "Ain't that right, Elvira?"

The giant mosquito's wings flap furiously. I'd be furious too if someone turned me into a mosquito.

"I still don't know what you want me to do," I say carefully. Whatever he wants, it's going to cost. "I'm game, though."

"That's the spirit," he says. "Ya see, I think the mosquito's pregnant, fulla eggs."

I lift the surprisingly heavy carrier up onto an examining table and walk around it like I see giant pregnant mosquitoes every day. "Well, they lay their eggs in water."

Smoot snorts.

"I have a dog bath. We could try that."

I fill the dog bath, which is a little less than three feet around, with six inches of water. Then we set the carrier with the mosquito beside it.

"Think this'll work, Elvira?" Smoot asks. That elicits two flaps of the wings. "Aha! That's a yes."

Without warning, he opens the front of the carrier, and out flies Elvira. She drones into the air, circles the clinic, then plops into the dog bath. She gets right to business, lowering herself into the water. Half an hour later, there's a clutch of light-brown eggs and she daintily climbs out.

"I'll take her home now and exchange her back into her own body. I owe you, sir. Perhaps you'd like to take your fee in the form of a five percent stake in my metamorpholyzer company. It's just startin' to make serious cash."

He takes the device out of his pocket again to show me and smiles. I'm shaking my head, thinking about my overdue rent, of trying for ten, maybe even fifteen percent.

There's a blink of light so bright it disorients me for a moment.

I run over to the dead cocker spaniel that's bagged and lying in the clinic corner. Nothing beats the scrumptious smell of freshly dead dog. I have a strong urge to pee on it. So I do.

"Disgusting," Smoot says. He grabs me by my collar and snaps on a leash. Then he shoves me into the carrier. "I suggest you work on your manners or you'll never get adopted at the pound."

Holy crap. I have a tail. I just peed on a dead dog.

Smoot mutters, "Killing Elvira's boyfriend Joe with your incompetence. Not that he didn't have it coming, knocking up Elvira. I brought her here to get around that new abortion law."

Now he's talking to what used to be me. "Feel a little younger, Doctor Cramdon? Sorry ya had be a dog, but that's over now. Worth every penny, right?"

I savor the fading dead dog smell as he lugs me out of the clinic.

Bob Calverley is the author of a sixties novel, *Purple Sunshine: Sex & Drugs, Rock & Roll, War, Peace & Love*; the murder mystery *Hyperventilated Underwater Blues*; and *Sunshine Blues*, a sequel to *Purple Sunshine*. He was an award-winning newspaper reporter and a writer, editor, and public relations consultant. In 1968–1969, he served in the 187th Assault Helicopter Company in Vietnam. He lives in Thousand Oaks, California.

TALES OF ATLANTIS SIX

Volume One: Act II—The Epiphany

Gabriel Fergesen

———————◦◇◦———————

These are the first two scenes of the second act of Tales of Atlantis Six. *It will be composed of four acts, each on a separate planet and in a separate century, but all within the same narrative.*

Scene I: The Sea

The frigid, turbulent water thundered against the scalding sand, frenetically frothed forward, then crept back to the devouring tides; the sea was silent. A wave yawned wide, colossal, and mounted a symmetric assault against the shore, followed by another, then another, then another, smiting the sand. Far from the shore, files of faintly enumerated crests stood silent in paradoxical stillness to the frenzied and incessant cacophony and violence at the shore.

Beneath the brilliant blue sky lay a village, neither particularly fashionable nor mundane but meticulously clean, its white-painted houses blindingly bright in the summer day, and silhouetted against it, a diminutive shadow on the empty shore, stood a boy watching the tide. He was dressed in blandly formal clothing, a white button-down shirt and pants of a nondescript grey, and his clean-shaven face, luminous with summer sunlight, gazed with a profound and resolute melancholy through the waves. He concentrated, countenance clenched with strain, stared forward once more, and watched, but saw only digits—the polyrhythms between crests, the angle at which each swell deteriorated to surges of white water and froth, the system of flow and recession that, composited, formed the sea's motion, *1,020 meters per second*—a cacophony of insignificance and nonsense. Yet, when he ceased to see, silencing the statistics, he heard the vast elemental aggression of the sea, the waves striking the shore, the briefest of instants passing from a symmetric eternity, the same moment eons before and eons after this second.

A fluting tone then began, harmonic, ethereal, and beauteous, swept upward, then vibrated through a variety of lows and into a brief climax; he recognized consonants, feminine, and perhaps, if he traced it closely, his name, shot with urgency . . .

"Avi, Avi, wake, *wake!* Wake, stand, *run*, your grandmother is dying—only these twelve minutes of life remain."

Avi's eyes flew open, and again his brain boiled with statistics. His glance flitted over her face, and after several seconds of incomprehension, he recognized the gene-tailor's daughter, the prodigy renowned throughout the City for her easy, seemingly incidental mastery of refitting flesh, sewing away disease, then shuddered with an irrepressible revulsion. There she—Edith—stood, a blonde-haired omen, pale countenance bound into stoic composure, her dun-color eyes traversing, probing, analyzing his face, and Avi leapt up hastily and ran.

His panicked cadence carried him from the shore and into symmetric grids of white, clean, cubic houses, the fierce summer radiance reflecting off the rows of identical, ornate brass doorknobs and onto the foot of a plaster monolith, a pale patch imposed on the horizon, jutting beyond the comparatively miniscule neighborhoods, its broad face marred with files of jet-black glass squares and one bronze plaque inscribed SANCTUARY. He throttled the intricate doorknob, flung open the mahogany door, dashed through the stark white foyer, hurtled across five flights of steel stairs. A series of practiced, instinctual strides led him through a labyrinth of embellished oak doors, so characteristic of the City, and left him panting before a metal panel, indicated as INVIGORATION—209 by white luminous letters blazing beside it. As Avi gestured cautiously, a small light flared green; the panel retracted, revealing a minute, gray chamber abruptly illuminated, and the corridor echoed with the periodic tone of motors, the steady trickling of liquid, and the shallow, throbbing hiss of pneumatics. This was a chamber no ordinary Citizen would enter, see, or know existed, the brutalism concealed beneath the Sanctuary's stucco exterior. But his grandmother, now lying in this ward, had been, for all her contrary, subversive, dissident gestures, essential to the City—the whispered rumors were indisputable evidence of that. Avi strode inside, the plate gradually sealed behind him, and before him, embedded in the deafening cacophony of machinery, lay an amalgamation, coffinlike, of white polycarbonate panels, each rising and sinking in some incoherent rhythm; set beneath it lay a blackened window, half reflecting the delirium of incessant, artificial labor she inhabited now—two hands clutching invisible oars, rowing exhaustedly across an infinite and virtual lake, the waves eerily synchronous and symmetric, the sky in perpetual twilight—and half displaying TREATMENT 501 OF 501– TIME REMAINING: 30 SECONDS. He comprehended fully that his grandmother's exertions were classified as *inadequate*, and as every fiber, nerve, bone, and vein was prodded, twisted, slit, sampled, and reconstructed, second after second irrevocably elapsed.

A siren's baying pierced the silence; the room resounded as the pneumatics accelerated. Avi felt the pounding cacophony of the mechanism penetrate his flesh, his muscles vibrate, and his heart rattle with the agonizing intensity of the sound. Beneath the panels already contracting to a coffin form, a display rapidly pulsed PALLIATIVE in red, a word he knew to indicate temporary resituation, and suddenly all was silent, still.

An unseen chime echoed, and a shallow, serene voice, female, lilted:

"Enlightening care complete. Patient has five minutes, thirty-two seconds before resolution."

The motors complained as the sparkling panels slowly pivoted from pale, scar-speckled skin toward the ceiling. The harsh brilliance of the ceiling fixture illuminated the regiments of dripping needles. Avi stared appalled at the crumpled, gaunt, glistening body—the skin punctuated with innumerable microscopic wounds—of his grandmother lying on the white polycarbonate, still breathing. Her eyelash twitched, a minute motion, and suddenly his grandmother, Eleanor, shot upright, trembling with resolve, gaze suffused with the intimacy and love she lacked the time to express. Her speech was accompanied by expressions of profound agony, as though every word was torn from her throat, but she still gagged out:

"This . . . City not *only*"—she broke into a spasm of coughing, then continued—"seek . . . preserve *outside* . . . truth both gift and *duty* . . . *sacrifice*"—here gesticulating feebly—"saves *many*." Remorse, apology, and guilt welled in her eyes, but could not annihilate the determination that permeated her face. What followed was a series of words enunciated and inflected with agonizing precision: "Community," and here Avi comprehended that Eleanor was addressing the omnipotent network, "disown Avi." She looked at him pleadingly, imploringly, but he now comprehended the vague allusions that saturated his youth, the inevitability of her action: It was considered improper to discuss it, yet there was an unspoken yet vast lease to remain and remain oblivious to what lay Outside the City. He . . . he now possessed neither parent nor Citizenship, and the lease to this dream would soon expire.

The intelligence drained from her eyes, replaced by a blank silence that subsided into profound and final sleep. Avi crossed, silently, soberly, heart thundering with concealed fury, to the steel panel, which quickly receded, descended the steel stairwell enumerating the nails that positioned the moldings, and stepped from the sanitary white lobby into the City's streets. He meandered on, hollow, with neither sentiment nor thought, his heart knotted and stopped. Above the symmetric, hueless houses, the horizon billowing in the heat, the firmament was unvaryingly blue, the sky seamless, claustrophobic. Mechanically, he paced off the weary distance, another insignificant figure musing on his demise, the streets perpetually occupied somehow vacant. Once, he saw a flitting, lithe shadow flicker across the asphalt, but he soon dispelled this phantom by classifying it as merely another manifestation of his insanity. The sun, Sol, soon blazed low in the sky, and before the shore, still luminous in the twilight sun, the street was shrouded in shadows.

Avi abruptly felt his stomach ache with hunger; halting, he strode to the nearest door, grasped its knob, and attempted to twist it. The knob was as immobile as stone. Discomfited, he turned to the three knobs near it, gleaming in the last light of the day, and found them equally rigid. He pounded at the door, panicking, and the only response was silence. Subduing his sudden spasm of paranoia, methodically he traversed from house to house, tested knob after knob, and found all equally inhospitable. Imposed against the distant shores, the plaster City, brilliant red in the receding light of the afternoon, remained impossibly vacant; he would freeze, starve, and expire in these symmetrical streets. Suppressing a limp, he proceeded grimly toward the sea; a rectangular darkness, a door-shaped vacancy in the air, abruptly unfurled before him. At once famished and terrified, Avi comprehended immediately that this passage, however ambiguous, led from his purgatory, and that his torment had been engineered to render this dark passage irrefusable. Hastily, he ran through the rectangular shadow into a long, lightless corridor that rang beneath his step; he saw the invisible threshold he had crossed seal suddenly, the sunset gleaming off some cyclopean form briefly, and some door open in the distance, a weaker, feebler luminescence, yet dashed desperately onward. Finally, he emerged into a mountainous plain dusted with iron-stained red sands beneath a darkened, cloud-spotted, but uniformly blue sky, and behind him noticed a crude and colossal dome structure constructed of concrete and metal supports with a section open. As he approached it, the section swung shut and sealed seamlessly, and all that remained of Avi's passage and the City of his birth was a flawless facet of the dome, a sheet of cement interspersed with steel. His hunger, awe, and horror overcame him, and Avi Montagnan, City-born, collapsed into the red sands of Terra.

Scene II: The Soil

He slowly, groggily awoke, moment by moment, and exhaustedly discerned some soft, furred fabric nestled about his body; an invigorating, perhaps comforting, warmth; an amber light flickering across the ceiling, which he soon noticed (not grammatical, but I adore the timing) was demarcated by regular, half-cylindrical bulges; and fantastical, extinct aromas he recognized only from his grandmother's cooking. Upon further examination, he noticed the walls exhibited the same pattern, that of stacked logs, and his eye was drawn to a hearth of a prehistoric make: a square stone column, hollow, flickering and flaring with fire, a log popping occasionally in the flame and throwing off showers of embers. He then heard a rough, coarse woman's voice, unexpectedly articulate.

"You haven't seen a chimney before, then—how mysterious, yet not nearly so as that a *child*, with the discernment of an infant, dressed in the pinnacle of eight thousand years' textiles, a garment woven from infinitesimal threads, both bland *and* casual, faints in the Heights and is left abandoned, prey to night and death!" The harsh yet benevolent frankness of her speech overwhelmed him, and Avi shivered. As he sat up and turned about, his eye was stopped by a winking series of lights, a red, luminous asterisk that converged on a gleaming sphere, the center of nearly half her face filled with steel. Appalled by this aberration, Avi lost his composure, and his eyes traversed from the central lights to an icon, discrete yet prominently stamped in the device: eight thin rays emerging from a circle, two repeated—the double-struck sun, the symbol of RITON Industries. The eye opposite it, however, was kind, wise, blue, and human, the nose natural, the lips smiling.

"An Integration," she explained. "Your gawking is natural; they're horrific disfigurements, but were once thought the *salvation* of humanity—technology that accelerated and amplified human ability to speeds beyond those of machinery, fusing intelligence with heightened functionality." She mused briefly and despondently, and Avi noticed the dust that had accumulated in various corners, conspicuous from the sterility of the City.

"You emerged from a civilization considered extinct; evidently you know *nothing* of these prior nine centuries— STATION, the Terran Businesses Coalition. We'll exchange histories, your origin for the modern world's. In the meantime, it would be despicable of me not to feed a starving child. How old are you? Twelve?"

"Marginally younger," Avi answered somewhat sulkily.

She walked briskly to a countertop, lit the wick of a nearby lamp, snatched several oblong, green zucchinis and a yellow squash from a basket, and tossed them on a wooden block. Avi saw one hand's fingers split, halves separating from long, flat blades, and the flesh sheaths slowly retract down, pivoting to rest against her palm, revealing five knives. As she discussed, her right hand twitched and tapped, translated by the blades into syncopated waves of motion, impossibly dexterous, chopping and dicing with incomprehensible speed and elegance.

"I'm Menih, an S6 Stationdweller in Lower Terra Orbit, a chef—all terms that mean nothing to you, I'm certain. This," she gestured around with her left, unknived hand, "is all I possess now, along with a garden that produces precisely enough food for our minute family to survive. The rent," a dismal, caustic resentment and strange weakness entered her voice, "for living on this lush planet, even in such a desolate *hole* as this, far outpaces my salary, but somehow we supply the funds to remain. This planet, Terra," she continued irately, perceiving the keen discomfort on Avi's face, "supposedly, as they phrased it, to preserve its *thousand thousand forms of life*, is now solely owned by the TBC, the Terran Businesses Coalition, and whatever sections of the planet are not termed preserves are now squalid, barren plots of land, for-rent deathbeds, bring-your-own-tent, intended for Station's wealthiest to lease something priceless: moments breathing an actual atmosphere, to feel the sun, to hear birdsong—things incomparable to the unfathomable, black, star-speckled absence of space."

"And as to Station," she continued, sober yet somewhat smilingly, as she swept the chopped vegetables into a pan, walked to the hearth, and set it atop the black kettle dangling in the flames, "it's a collection of all the fools, workers, parents, and subtrillionaires, almost half Integrated or Illuminated—genetically modified—the majority of humanity who, over five decades of steady increases, eventually couldn't pay their lease, were evicted and jettisoned into space so that either they'd deplete the surplus population or enter the accumulation of stray craft docked together, a heap of ships that functioned as a *de novo*—improvised—space station."

Attempting to comprehend this bizarre history, his stomach clenched with starvation, Avi clung to his composure, and appeared only mildly perplexed. Suddenly he interjected, "But why, then, did you construct anything if this is only a temporary residence?"

For an instant, Menih's relentlessness faltered, and Avi saw beneath her smile agony, anguish, loneliness, and inexorable courage. She ran to the pot carrying a plate, lifted the pan, and sifted its sizzling contents onto the plate, then handed it and some silverware to Avi.

Menih spoke deliberately, stoically. "Come outside; I will show you the truth beneath this." She gripped a faded rag, dragged a white bar across it, ran the blades across the rag, submerged them in a bowl, and flicking off the water, let her fingers reconstitute, then stepped through a plastic curtain. Avi followed, emerged into brilliance and, squinting, discerned he stood on a plane. Though darkened, the sun stood centered in the sky, casting shallow light across the narrow plateau, a brief respite from a broad, steep path cut from the otherwise unmarred twisting, mountainous ground. As Menih and Avi walked into the hot, dry air, he noticed something unsettling: a silhouette, still against the horizon, arms akimbo, until it slowly receded.

Menih then spoke slowly and solemnly. "Forgive me for what I've done, Avi. You understand I deplore Integrations, but these were *necessary*. My children are both Integrated— their blood didn't function. It kept them alive, but it couldn't *breathe* enough. On Station, oxygen is limited, precious."

She collected her breath, stood silent several moments, then continued, her words periodically punctuated with sobs. "The atmosphere there is 18.7 percent oxygen, only slightly above the concentration required for life, too low for infants, and especially one with faulty blood—anemia. It is our custom to supply these first breaths, oxygen price disregarded, to infants, with no reward but that freely given. I had three children, two boys and one girl, lying beneath the acrylic dome of the incubator, screaming noiselessly for the right to breathe, crying for air, and I saw in the doctors' gentleness, the solemnity, the silence of that moment that I was to decide. My children, *all anemic*, would die if they remained aboard, stifled before they comprehended what it was to live or after having slowly matured, insufficiently oxygenated, in space, decaying in their youth as bones malformed, muscles weakened, their mind shriveled, and their bodies collapsed—I had seen it before."

"They still live, though I knew the death I could have condemned them to. I reached up, gripped and twisted open the oxygen valve, watched the dome cloud as their breath continued, and a nurse, observing my decision, handed me a silver canister, enough to perpetuate their life one month—the standard supply for anemic infants. She said only one phrase: "*Good luck*.""

They approached a fence constructed from wooden sheets, although Avi noticed they were crudely hewn, bearing axe marks, and Menih located one leaning against the others sunk into the soil and placed it aside, revealing life, verdant: a thousand curling shoots, vivid blossoms scattered throughout, and an interlacing vine with yellow, knobbed gourds at its tips.

"The lung Integrations were as horrific as you might imagine," Menih began, somewhat tonelessly. "After the births, it was discovered that their bodies were still too inefficient to survive even in Terra's atmosphere, and that we needed to accelerate their respiration—breathing," she explained woefully.

"The surgeries began in haste. There was only one month until the children, my daughter and my sons, would begin to deteriorate, so I let them be lifted from the incubator—their oxygen masks first pressurized—placed, backs exposed, on an operating table. A drill bored through their ribs, a duct slid into each opened cavity, and a small valve fastened into the flesh. My children live, however," she declared.

As Avi contemplated this tragedy, he walked into the garden, Menih following closely behind. Before a thousand leaves fluttering in the breeze, standing on ground spotted with tufts of foliage, Avi noticed three children far from the gate. They stooped, wearing brightly hued, faded clothes (hollow colors), something periodically extending and retracting from their backs. Their shovels flew upward, then descended into the soil, and Avi heard the labor in their breath. They stood, wholly absorbed, until Menih called to them with a condescension approaching gentleness, "Elian, Ciryn, Reln, you have a visitor . . ."

The shortest of the three, whom Menih called Ciryn, turned about and bounded, periodically leaping, toward Avi—an inexplicably euphoric, chaotic motion—fluttering black fabric pipes unfurling, winglike, from her back periodically. Avi saw the indescribable innocence that suffused her gaze, the ecstasy of life, unmarred, and vowed silently to defend it.

Gabriel Fergesen is seventeen and has attended no classes on creative writing, but he has been working independently to read some of the world's greatest novels by his high school graduation.

Robots, Robots, It's All Robots, his first book, was self-published at age six and earned him a live interview with the Huffington Post. *Tales of Atlantis Six*, an experiment in combining science fiction and character-driven epic fantasy, began as a short story, "Act I: The Timeless," written at age thirteen. He is currently pursuing a publisher for the full novel.

Gabriel Fergesen is currently his robotics team's primary programmer, conducts molecular biology and renewable energy research with a Caltech team, is a leader in his church, and is working on his Eagle project. He hopes to be accepted to a college to study mathematics, access all the sciences, and periodically write novels.

ROBOTS

Mark Frankcom

I'll call them Paul and Adam in this story—not their real names. They crawled through the air-conditioning ducting to the large building.

"Where are we going?" whispered Adam.

"To the HQ building. They control everything from there. All their computer systems. We'll blow it all up." Paul felt for the sticks of dynamite in his belt.

"Why?"

"If we take out their computer, then all their robots and drones will die. It's as simple as that."

"I see. Is that a good idea?"

"It's the only way to stop them," grunted Paul. "They control everything now. Especially the robots. They are everywhere. We have to do this. Not far now." He shimmied forward. "Stay quiet now."

"OK," answered Adam.

They emerged into the central utility room. It was lit by bright neon lights, which almost blinded them after the darkness of the duct.

"The computer center is directly above us. We'll place the charges here."

"Won't the blast kill us?" asked Adam.

"We should be OK in the duct. Cover your mouth and eyes. There will be a lot of dust."

Paul set the charge and lit a long fuse. He pulled Adam back to the duct. "Get in there. Hurry."

The noise was deafening.

The computer was completely destroyed.

Paul felt odd.

Adam shut his eyes. He didn't say a word.

Then Paul's mind went blank.

All the robots had shut down.

Mark Frankcom is a British author living in California. His first novel, *Sold!*, and its sequel, *The Return*, were published on Amazon. In 2023, he combined the two books under one title, *The Baumann Chronicles*.

He also enjoys writing books for children. His first, *Bear in the Pocket,* was followed by three more.

Mark's wife, Margret, also an author of children's books, is German, and they have three children.

The Frankcoms are both very involved with nonprofit organizations that support disabled or mentally challenged children.

WHAT WAS THAT?

Alex Holub

———————————◇◇◇————————————

"Jim! Jim! Wake up!" whispers his wife. "Someone's downstairs."

"Huh? What?" Jim had just made a hole in one at the club's annual golf outing. He rubs the sleep from his eyes and sits up.

The bedside clock reads 2:18 a.m.

"It's probably the cat trying to catch that imaginary mouse."

"No, it's louder than that. Listen."

Jim hears the wind whistling through the eaves and a branch from the oak tree scraping against the window. "I don't hear anything." He's pulling up the covers when there's a loud thump and the unmistakable sound of breaking glass. "What was that?" Jim yells, leaping out of bed.

"It's what I've been trying to tell you. There's someone downstairs."

Jim pulls his shotgun and box of shells from the closet. "Stay here and call the police," he says, heading for the stairs. Jim is planting his foot on the first step when his wife races from the bedroom.

"They . . . they said they'd be right here."

"Good."

"Don't you think you should wait?"

"And be robbed blind before they get here? No way. I'm going to teach whoever it is not to mess with James T. Walker."

Jim's moving cautiously when his slipper catches on the runner, pitching him head over heels down the stairs. The shotgun discharges into the ceiling, sending powdery chunks of plaster raining down.

"Jim! Jim! Are you all right?" his wife yells as she runs down the stairs.

At the same time, there's a loud knock on the door. "Open up! It's the police."

Jim's wife climbs over his crumpled body and heads for the door. "I'm coming! I'm coming!" she yells.

Jim's climbing to his feet, using the shotgun for support, when two cops rush in holding flashlights and drawn pistols. One shields Jim's wife while the second cop grabs the shotgun, sending Jim toppling onto the steps. "Stay right there," says the cop, pointing his gun at Jim's crumpled form.

"Don't shoot," yells Jim's wife. "That's my husband."

"But we heard a shot," says the older cop.

"I know. Sometimes my husband's a little clumsy. He fell down the stairs and the shotgun went off."

"Why was he carrying a loaded shotgun?"

"We thought we heard someone down here."

"Well, I'm sure if anyone was here, they're long gone," says the older cop holstering his gun.

The second cop helps Jim to his feet. "Sorry for the misunderstanding."

"That's OK, but please search the house."

"No problem," says the older cop. "Ted, you take that side of the house. I'll check the living and dining rooms."

Jim and his wife are sitting on the bottom step, huddled together, when they hear raucous laughter coming from the dining room. "Ted, come here. You've gotta see this."

The laughter continues as the two cops walk out of the dining room carrying a round, black object. "Do you recognize this?"

Jim and his wife stare sheepishly at the object. "It's our new robovac," says Jim.

The cop hands Jim the vacuum. "You might want to reprogram that thing so it doesn't start cleaning at two in the morning."

Jim hears the older cop say, "Wait till the guys at the station hear about this," as the front door slams shut.

Alex Holub was a corporate executive, long-time business owner, and full-time fiction writer since retiring five years ago. His short stories run the genre gamut from children to humor to horror—all with twist endings.

He is working on a novel featuring an offbeat independent contractor (detective) whose business card reads: WHATEVER IT TAKES.

Alex lives with his wife and two cats in Moorpark, California.

STATE ROUTE 733

Hal T. Horowitz

The white lines darted by the bus as it headed north on state Route 733. Benjamin August leaned his head against the window, losing himself in the reflection of an occasional vehicle. Cars slid through the bus as though not cars at all, but phantoms whose images were there and then gone as they disappeared into the haze of a graying dusk. A dusty brown two-door sedan passed, then pulled in front of the bus.

He'd been on this road with Melissa. The soft rolling hills were more scenic then. Sometimes, she'd drive up here alone in her convertible to get away from him for a few days. Not often. Just when he'd hurt her.

"Ladies and gentlemen," the driver announced over his intercom, "we're expecting rain and icy conditions tonight. We'll be spending the night at the Summit Inn, if conditions warrant." Benjamin looked up toward the foreboding sky. It would rain and the road would ice up, but the bus would not stop for the night. He was sure.

Benjamin saw Melissa in the rear of the bus. *When had SHE gotten on?* They exchanged the quick, awkward smiles of former lovers who didn't plan to meet, then he quickly averted his attention back to the window.

Everyone on the highway was either going to or coming from someplace; whenever Benjamin caught a glimpse of another vehicle's passengers, he wondered which. Sometimes he thought he actually knew.

The road ran straight along this stretch of highway, with so moderate an incline as to be imperceptible. It lent itself easily to speeding. Route 733 was known for the many deaths it had witnessed over the years.

Farther on, he saw a lone figure, a hitcher, wrapped in a fleece-lined denim jacket, his thumb signaling his need. As the bus drew nearer, Benjamin could see the hitchhiker's breath hanging heavy in the cooling air. The dusty sedan began to slow. Its driver eased past the hitcher and checked him out, then came to a full stop, just far enough ahead of him to make him run for his ride. As the bus approached, Benjamin watched the hitcher say something through a half-open window. He knew the conversation verbatim.

"How far ya' goin'?"

"Just over the pass."

"No problem. Hop in." The driver pulled back onto the road behind the bus. "Been hitchhikin' long?"

"Since Danburg." The hitcher swiped back a long wisp of hair that had fallen over his brow. "Mind if I smoke?"

The driver slid open the ashtray. It was filled with crumpled ash and broken butts. "Got an extra?"

"Help yourself." The passenger would shake three caramel-colored filter tips through the opening in the red-and-white cellophane pack and offer them to his host.

"Thanks." He lit up. "Live in Danburg?"

"No."

"Just visitin'?"

"You could say that."

"Looks like rain."

The hitcher would eye the darkening sky and agree. "Yeah."

Then the car would drop from sight until they sped past the bus.

Benjamin felt a mild jerk as the driver dropped the bus into a lower gear, slowing it slightly as the incline increased gently up into the hills. The edge of the road was lined with thickets of white oak, thick, sturdy trees with nearly bare branches shooting out almost from their trunks, many as thick themselves as trunks of smaller trees. Their crowns were the amber and orange of the season.

"What's yer name, friend?" the driver asked after an uncomfortable silence.

"You got any money?"

"Beg yer pardon?"

"Money! You got any money?"

"No. No money." He would edge over and slow. "This is far enough, pal."

"Nice watch," the hitchhiker would say. "I'll take it."

"You can let yerself out right here, pal." Then he'd see the cold glint of a steel barrel in the hitcher's hand. "What's that?"

"Just give me the watch."

The bus passed the car again. In it, despite the nearing full darkness of the encroaching night, Benjamin knew there was a struggle, and despite the growing distance following the passage, he would recognize the sharp crack of a handgun.

"Oh no. Whadja hafta go an' do that fer?" That was all Benjamin would know the driver said as the bus continued up the hill.

The hitcher would slide the watch off a limp wrist, pull the body out the wide driver's door, and drag it into the stands of oak standing sentry along state Route 733. Benjamin knew all of this. Moments later, the dusty car sped past the bus once more and disappeared into the dusk ahead.

Benjamin glanced back at Melissa. He missed her. He was little—no, he was nothing without her. There had been another woman, but she wasn't the reason. He just wasn't one for commitments. He was never sure if he loved Melissa but that hadn't stopped him from telling her on so many occasions that he did. The other woman meant nothing, just a lark, the final hurt. But Melissa had been good to him, and now it tore deeply that he had hurt her as he had. Now he was moving on, running from a past like so many others on the highway, just moving on from one place to the next.

A sliver of pink sunset, the last vestige of day, hidden behind some low, broken clouds, found a crack in the heavy overcast, then crept beneath a saddle between two hills. Then the world turned a dark gray. Benjamin's world was always dark gray.

He listened to the road hum beneath the ponderous bus as it trudged up the increasing incline, now surrendering itself to gentle curves that flowed with the hills alongside. The oaks were below them now, their beautiful crowns waiting to shed themselves of their amber and orange leaves he'd just seen from below, just waiting for that first autumn freeze.

Small beads of drizzle began to dot the window. This was the beginning. He looked rearward. Trailing the bus, two headlamps caused the road to glow. As they grew brighter, Benjamin knew they would divide and then, like a magnet, draw back together. They drew nearer to the bus and split apart, one slightly forward of the other. A couple of stupid kids on motorcycles, their dark leather jackets glittering from the drizzle, shot past the bus, one on the right, the other on Benjamin's left. "Idiots," he thought. "They'll kill themselves when the road ices up."

Benjamin forced his jaw downward to alleviate the sudden plug of air in his ears that muted the sound of the bus and blurred any ambient noise.

Splat!

Sound returned to him.

Splat, splat!

Larger, noisier rain began to pelt his window. One of the bikes began to weave, but it would right itself and disappear around one of the road's less gentle curves, appear again for a moment, then dip down, swallowed into the highway itself as its roar diminished.

Whack, whack!

Benjamin startled as the driver set the bus's windshield wipers in motion.

The bus slowed to negotiate a sharp turn, and then another, even sharper, as the hills surrendered themselves to a rockier terrain. Water began to run rearward in rivulets. Benjamin watched. The bus slowed again as its wheels tried to gain purchase on the now increasing incline.

And then it would be night.

The rear of the bus skidded slightly. Benjamin waited for its engine's hum to become a whine as soon as the driver downshifted. He knew a deep ravine, appearing from nowhere, would now parallel the road and travel the course of the bus, widening, then narrowing, then widening again as it wished.

A blast of red filled the bus. Benjamin's hands, the backs of the seats in front of him, the rear of the driver's cap: crimson, all crimson. Two flashing emergency lights outside his window announced its source, an ambulance.

He saw the motorcycle on its side, a wet tarp fully covering the body alongside it. The other bike stood parked off the road, its rider holding his face in his hands. The bus edged slowly by.

The road glistened from the freezing rain. Benjamin craned his neck to see ahead. Headlights revealed four wheels facing skyward, one still spinning slowly, glowing from thin patches of ice. A bleeding arm, sheathed in the torn sleeve of a fleece-lined denim jacket, lay extended from a window beneath the crushed roof. Black skid marks, slowly being frozen over, bore testimony to a violent crash. A small flame flickered from its chassis, emitting the rank odor of burnt rubber and the faint smell of seeping gasoline.

Benjamin watched the wreckage pass and shrink into a small red glow. He looked around. Melissa watched it from the rear window. The man with the red-stained jacket seemed disinterested. A young man with a leather biker jacket shed a single tear. Benjamin hadn't noticed him aboard before.

Shadowy mountains would soon rise from the earth to the right of the bus, and to its left, the slope would fall into a black abyss. Route 733 slowly twisted and curved its way once again into a steady drizzle. Benjamin could again see the white dashes that separated traffic glisten and then become part of the past.

A convertible, its top down, sat rusting in the rain, its long white hood crushed against a boulder of near-equal size. Benjamin knew. He knew she had driven up here alone, just days ago. It had been tears then, not rain, that would have streaked her softly rounded cheeks. He had hurt her again. He wanted to comfort her, to go to her and take her in his arms and tell her that everything would be all right. He looked at his new gold watch as if it could foretell whether there was still time enough for apologies and promises. There wasn't. She would just have to hurt.

A thin haze of sunlight lit the rear of the bus. Melissa seemed to glow in it as the convertible slowly melted into the horizon. *Was it dawn already?*

"It looks like the weather is clearing, folks," the bus driver announced, passing a motel at the summit.

The sharp curves gave way to a gentle arc in the road. Benjamin suddenly realized that the windshield wipers had stopped. The ragged dark clouds had softened and assumed the silver edge of a warming sun rising barely moments after it had set.

Benjamin could see the slight incline of a straight, dry road, the sun suddenly above and darkening clouds ahead. The glass reflected the few passing cars, their images seeming to glide smoothly through the bus. They were not cars. They were phantoms, phantom vehicles that had already traversed state Route 733. He watched as the white lines that separated the lanes disappeared beneath the bus. Everyone on the road was either going to or coming from somewhere. He, too, was running away. Running from commitment to a different forever. Forever was too long a time. *Nothing could last forever, could it?*

"Is anyone sitting there?" Melissa asked, pointing to the empty seat next to him. She smiled and sat down before he answered. She leaned her tangled golden hair against his fleece-lined denim jacket and took his arm in both her hands. "Think it will rain?" she asked.

"It'll rain." He smiled back. "Comfortable?"

"Mm-hmm."

"Me, too."

He leaned his head against the window.

The bus driver announced the possibility of rain and ice tonight and said something about stopping if conditions got too bad.

He couldn't remember boarding the bus and wasn't sure when he was supposed to get off.

A dusty brown two-door sedan passed by. There was a hitchhiker alongside the road ahead.

Benjamin looked again at his watch. His unadorned hand extended from the fleece-lined sleeve of his denim jacket. Benjamin knew he had made a commitment. He chose state Route 733.

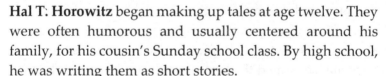

Hal T. Horowitz began making up tales at age twelve. They were often humorous and usually centered around his family, for his cousin's Sunday school class. By high school, he was writing them as short stories.

Hal was born in Chicago and came to Los Angeles with his parents in 1954, at age ten. He was a business administration major and peppered his studies with courses in journalism, art, and creative writing. Hal returned to college after his discharge from the air force in 1963. He had a thirty-two-year career in commercial finance and equipment leasing, followed by a second career of twenty-two years as a bank recruiter, career counselor, and EQ mentor, during all of which he continued to try to improve his writing craft.

He has written numerous business articles for a variety of trade newspapers and magazines, and has had his short story *The Cemetery Picnics* selected for publication as an "Outstanding Writing" in the 1997 California Writers Club, San Fernando Valley anthology, *Down in the Valley*. He has also written and contributed to numerous plays and skits for private organizations and groups.

Now retired, Hal is devoting his full attention to caring for his wife, Barbara, and writing. He is optimistic about seeing his most recent work, a five-generation family saga titled *Forward tho' I cannot see*, published by the end of 2023.

LIGHT WITHOUT FLAMES

Jeanne Rawlings

The night wind swept through the woods like an axe, sheering off icicles and sending their frozen ghosts into the village. On the edge of the forest where the pines began, an old fir tree stood. It was the tallest of trees and looked down on a clearing where, only hours before, a short, pretty pine tree had been. The old man and a little boy had done it. Cut it and left a stump behind.

In the peak branches of the majestic fir, the raven sat preening his beak. "You will always be a Solstice tree," the black bird said, "and you should thank the gods for that."

"A Christmas tree," the needles whistled.

"Solstice tree, Solstice tree!" the bird cawed, holding on as the trunk swayed. It was his home base, the refuge of his ancestors.

The bickering always began in the season when the sun was small and winter set in. "This darkness is a sign," the raven warned. "The craziness is coming!"

The fir usually stood silent, a black arrow against the gray sky. But that night, the storm gave its thoughts sound and the needles vibrated. "You fear people, but I'm glad for them, even with their sharp saws and axes."

Like every tree on the mountain, it was grounded in the ways of all the rooted ones; it had no fear. As the wind gave it movement, its questions began. "Tell me again about the beauty in the village. And the splendor of Christmas trees."

Such inquiry made no sense to the raven. He knew the damage done by people, which the tree had no idea about because it could not travel. But he was a loyal bird, and after all he had wings, and his friend did not. So he usually gave in and relayed what he'd seen from above.

"Do you mean the metal fruit they put on their limbs? And the silver that drips without melting? The balls that hold the light without flames? It's all true."

Over many years, he brought back descriptions of Solstice lights in the streets and decorations inside that he spied from the windowsills. But the stories always ended with the dismal fate of the fallen Christmas trees. How their vibrant green turned brown, and how they were dragged out of the houses by their trunks, brittle and fire ready.

The tree did not cry. It never did. "Oh, to be chosen to celebrate the birth of the Creator!"

"Creator?" The bird flitted to a higher twig to make his point. "No, they celebrate one god! Ra! The one with the hawk's vision! Ra, who conquers the great winter night! The others are silly and confused. They worship a featherless child!"

"God coming into the world as a helpless human somehow," the tree countered.

"Helpless! And while they call it God's day, they spend all of the day giving gifts to one another. It's all muxed up! All of it is squirrel mites. Rubbish!"

"Mixed, not muxed. They're mixed up, like you. Confused about how to honor such an unimaginable time. The Son of God arriving at night. Just imagine!"

"There we agree. A god who wears the sun for a crown," the bird chattered on. "Ra! Ra!" Just saying the Egyptian name thrilled him as he clung to the branch with his claws. But the fir tree didn't answer.

"You're alive and should thank Ra you're too big to be stuffed into a house. Ra is everlasting, like you with your green leaves."

"Ah no," the tree moaned. "I'm not everlasting."

"Yes, you are." The raven hopped back and forth along the limb. "Evergreen! Ever! Ever!" He hopped when he charmed, which was always his answer for those he disagreed with. The tree merely rustled, until a gust of wind took hold and it spoke.

"Will you try again? To bring me an ornament that holds the light without flames?"

"If I remember. I might find it after the party's over, hanging on your friends in the trash."

The wind died down and the snow fell straight, quieting both the bird and the tree. Soon, protected by the needles, one tucked his head under his wing and dozed in his own warmth.

"They're not honoring Ra," the tree whispered before the snowflakes stilled its voice. "Not Saturn or any sort of god like that," it murmured. "They're honoring the One who was born when all the world was dark."

The raven began winter survival that night. The quarrel and the tinsel were forgotten. Then came the spring and nesting. And then came the fire.

Those who couldn't flee hid beneath the ground. Rabbits were especially champions at this and became the witnesses, explaining how the raven stayed until the flames stopped at the foot of the tree. Only after the bird flew off did the fire rear up like a horse and shake its red embers into the branches and across to the pines beyond.

There was a time of endless night, when the red sky turned black with ash and smoke. People arrived with axes, chasing the fire, trampling the earth overhead, tempting rabbits to run from their holes. They wouldn't get far on burned feet, but still, one raced out and got caught by a kind-hearted firefighter. He carried the story of the fire to his rabbit cousins in the village.

It wasn't until the second week that the raven returned. Bleakness replaced the quilt of green forest. He crested the ridgeline and wheeled in the sky, taking in the old landmarks that were now sores in the black fur of the forest. The tree lay on the hillside, as bare and bristly as a ribcage. Ravens do weep, and he landed on it and cawed and wept. There were no needles to catch the wind, and the tree did not answer.

The forest recovered miraculously. As the plants sprouted, the rabbits survived on their roots without killing them. They drank water from the creek, though the foxes and cats were as terrible as flames and just as unpredictable. While nothing looked the same, family making went on. Everyone found ways to rebuild: the birds, squirrels, foxes, and picas, too. And in January, the raven brought a little sparkly something he had rescued from the trash and sat with it in the bones of the old fir tree.

Over the years, the rabbit cousins reported that the old man and the boy from the village searched other parts of the mountain for their Christmas tree. While the forest grew back, the man shrank to the thickness of a child, until one day he didn't leave his house at all.

That December, a tree cutter entered the forest. Being social and sharing as rabbits are, the word from the village was that this was the old man's ghost, but the raven recognized him as the boy, grown up.

He landed in front of the young man as he walked, but when he got near, the raven flitted away. The villager laughed and followed until he tired of the game and turned around. But the bird shrieked and cawed. "This looks familiar," the man said, recognizing the place where he'd been with his father. They came to a stand of firs, a dozen saplings at least. In the middle, a tall, straight one glittered with broken ornaments. When the raven landed on a nearby tree and cawed, that was the one the young man cut down.

Every year, the villager returned. He tended the fir, removed broken ornaments, and secured a new ball on a limb before setting off to find a Christmas tree. But the creatures agreed there was only one true Solstice Christmas tree. Its ornaments held light without flames, so high that only a bird could reach them. And on Christmas Eve, it spoke while the raven listened.

Jeanne Rawlings is a former writer for National Geographic television, ABC television, and the Discovery Channel. As a producer, sound recordist, and photographer, she traveled the world researching and writing many documentary films. She was nominated for five Emmy Awards, won two Emmys, and received dozens of national film awards before retiring.

Jeanne grew up in Maryland and received her bachelor's degree in English from Frostburg State University. She went on to write short stories, published nonfiction magazine articles, and edited several published memoirs, as well as an art history book.

Blog: https://www.mywisdomroad.com/

GOING TO POT

J. Schubert

———————————⋄◈⋄———————————

Sure, times are bad, but the grass ain't greener anywhere else. I was speaking with Bud, whose opinion is "America is going to pot—I'm afraid we're having a decline of the American empire."

What a dope. I'm tired of all these pessimists. We live in the most powerful, influential country on Earth. What would the world do without our Levi's or sneakers? That's genuine fashion.

We can get whatever we want, whenever—right now. Sometimes free, America's favorite word. If you have the munchies, you've got a choice of any number of fast-food establishments and can get in and out in minutes. What kind of decline is that?

Aunt Mary says we won't be producing much anymore. That Americans will just be buyers. So what? A third of the economy is consumer spending. As long as we can buy what we want, it can't hurt.

Saudi Arabia used to be the number one producer of oil in the world. Know who's top dog now? Boom! Us. We've left them in the dust. Dinkie-dow.

Green Goddess worries about the national debt. Bo-Bo says it will catch up with us sooner than later. Good giggles.

A billion. Twenty-nine trillion. What's the difference? The government just prints more money to pay for it. Isn't that how we live anyway, kicking our problems down the road? How many times has the national debt been increased? The last time we were in the black was during the Clinton administration. Everyone got a surplus check; we didn't need a tax and debt increase to get it.

America going to pot? No, we're flying high. Fire it up. I'm going for all my freebies on 420.

———————◦◇◇◦———————

Andrew Erskine, a.k.a. J. Schubert, grew up in Santa Monica and makes his home in Southern California.

He earned a BA in English and American literature. He writes creative nonfiction and poetry. A recurrent theme in his work centers on the human condition.

THE ROCK

Theresa Schultz

The freshman class at Lincoln High was dismissed early. Students wandered around the campus deciding what to do.

"Hey, Sadie, would you like to take a hike on Blackberry Hill?" George asked.

"Sure," I need the exercise," she answered.

Sadie liked it when George took her hand as they climbed. It was her secret that she'd had a crush on him. She had told no one.

"I think I need to rest," Sadie said, reaching to sit on a large rock near the path.

"Me too." George knelt next to her. They looked at each other and giggled.

George leaned in front of Sadie and cupped her face in his hands, then gently kissed her. They couldn't stop giggling. It was a first kiss for both of them. That was the beginning of a romance that continued throughout their high school days. They often hiked on Blackberry Hill and stopped to rest on the familiar rock.

After graduation, George joined the navy. Although his letters were comforting, Sadie felt his presence when she sat on the large rock.

The day came when George was finally out of the service. After being together again for only a few hours, George said, "I'd like to walk up to 'our rock'."

Sadie perched on the rock, much like when she was fifteen. Again, George knelt next to her, reached into his pocket, and clutched a rock in his hand. The rock was a diamond. "Sadie, I love you so much. Will you marry me?"

They lived in the small town also named Blackberry Hill, and through the years, they often hiked to the rock with their three children. Sometimes it would include a picnic.

It was in the fall when George came home from work and announced he had important news. It was necessary for his job that they move to California.

Sadie immediately thought about leaving the rock. But how could she be concerned about a rock? It was only a rock. George's job was certainly top priority.

Two months later, a moving van was parked in front of their new home in California. They anxiously waited as their furniture was being unloaded. It took two husky men to load a heavy box onto a dolly.

"Where do you want this?" one asked.

"Leave it in the front yard," George said.

"What's that?" Sadie asked.

"Just open it."

The whole family shared hugs and tears when they saw the rock. It became a conversational piece in the neighborhood, even with strangers. Later, the great-grandchildren referred to it as "Nany's Rock."

It was seventy years after Sadie first sat on the rock when George had the rock engraved with Sadie's name. Once again it was moved.

George often knelt next to the rock as he placed flowers on Sadie's grave.

————⊸⬥⬦⬦⬥⊶————

Theresa Schultz has been a real estate agent in Thousand Oaks, California, for over thirty years, and has authored three books:

Dear God, I'm Divorced
It's Like . . . What Every Real Estate Agent Should Know
It's a Happy Face Day (a children's book)
Her books can be seen on her website:
www.val-ubooks.com
Her style of writing is to say a lot in a few words. Theresa has a blog, and posts something new every Monday. https://www.pswriters.org/theresa-schultz

THE THANKSGIVING VISIT

Marcia Smart

———————————◦◇◆◇◦———————————

Anna poked the last of the stuffing into the turkey and washed her hands at the sink. Wiping them on a towel, she glanced at the clock when she heard the doorbell ring.

"Eight a.m. on Thanksgiving morning. Who on earth can that be? Finish up your breakfast, kids, while I get the door." Anna couldn't help but giggle at the obvious pleasure her children took devouring their bowls of frosted cereal—a rare treat only allowed on holidays.

She opened the door to find a grinning old man standing on the porch.

"Dad! What on earth are you doing here?" She looked past him. "Is Mom with you? Come in, come in, you'll catch your death standing out there in the freezing cold."

Her father, Henry, gingerly crossed the threshold and stood in the foyer. "Nope. Just me."

"But why are you here now? Not that I'm not always glad to see you, but you and Mom aren't due to come for dinner until this afternoon. Here, let me hang your coat in the closet."

"No need. I'll put it here on the bench. I won't be staying long. Just wanted some alone time with my family. Is that all right?"

"Of course, Dad. Come into the kitchen. I just made a fresh pot of coffee."

Henry followed Anna to the kitchen, lingering at the wall of family photos displayed down the hallway.

Anna heard Henry's sigh from inside the kitchen. Smiling, she poured him a mug of hot coffee. "Look who's here, kids: Grandpa."

"Hey, Gramps," said Sara, the fifteen-year-old, barely looking up from her smartphone.

"Hi Grmmmph," sixth grader Mickey garbled through a spoonful of cereal.

"Grandpa!" Eight-year-old Marylou jumped off her chair and grasped Henry in her version of a bear hug.

"I can always count on my Lulu for the best hugs in town." He held her close and stroked her head before she wiggled free and returned to the table.

Henry walked over to Sara. "Got a little squeeze for old Gramps?"

Sara put the phone down, never leaving it out of her grasp. "Of course I do. You're the bomb, Gramps." She looked up at him with a huge smile.

Henry stared into her eyes, tears in his. "So pretty. Just like your momma when she was young. Wish I could see you walk down the aisle someday like I did her."

Sara crinkled her face. "That's a loooong way off, Gramps. But don't worry, you'll be first on the guest list." She picked up the phone and resumed her texting.

Henry turned his wistful gaze to Mickey. "And how about you, buddy? Too big for a hug?"

Mickey slurped up the last of the milk in his bowl and wiped away the thin mustache of white over his lip. "Yeah, kinda. High five?" Mickey held up his open palm.

Henry ignored the gesture. "Aww c'mon. You can humor your old Gramps." He moved in for a quick embrace, then stepped back and winked. "Won't be too many more of them as you get older."

"So, where's Mike?" Henry asked Anna. "Still upstairs sleeping?"

Anna pushed the coffee mug toward her father. "No. He's out playing a rousing game of Turkey Day touch football with his pals."

"Too bad. I was hoping to see him. That's a fine man you got there, Anna. It's an honor to be his father-in-law. You tell that to him for me, won't you?"

"What a nice thing to say. But you can tell him yourself. He should be back within the hour. How about a bagel or muffin while you wait?"

Henry took a long look around the cozy room, committing every inch to his mind. "Nope. Can't wait. Really gotta go now." He turned to leave the kitchen.

"But you just got here. And you haven't touched your coffee."

Henry was halfway down the hall when Anna caught up to him.

"Dad, what's the rush? Stay until Mike gets home. Mom probably doesn't even know you're gone."

Henry let out another deep sigh. "Oh . . . she knows."

He grabbed his coat from the bench. Anna held it up for him. He took his time putting it on, then turned to face his daughter. Tears filled his eyes. He placed his hand on her cheek. "You've been the most wonderful daughter, Anna, and mother and wife. I'm so proud to be your dad."

"Why, thank you, Daddy. I'm proud to be your daughter too."

She flashed him a smile, then gave him a hug.

He held her close, then opened the door and stepped out into the cold. At the top of the steps, he turned to look at her once more and blew her a farewell kiss.

Anna returned the gesture. "Be careful driving home. Looks like it's going to snow."

"Don't worry about me." Henry said. "I'm going home on angel's wings."

He winked and walked down the steps.

Anna shook her head. Daddy and his expressions. A few minutes later she was in the kitchen, judiciously carrying the cumbersome turkey roasting pan toward the oven, when the phone rang.

"Now what?" Setting it on top of the stove, she reached for the phone, heard her mother's voice talking to someone in the background.

"Mom? You there? What's up? Are you talking to Dad? How did he get home so fast?"

"What are you talking about, Anna? That's why I'm calling. Daddy's here with me at the hospital. The ambulance brought him in about two hours ago. Oh, Anna."

Her mother began crying loudly.

"Mom? Mom, I don't understand. Hospital? No, Daddy was just here. He left less than ten minutes ago."

"Anna, I don't know what you mean. Your dad has had a heart attack, and . . . oh Anna . . . he didn't make it." Henry's wife let out another wail. "He passed away about thirty minutes ago."

Anna fell into the closest chair. She looked at the clock. Eight thirty a.m. Thirty minutes ago her father was here in this kitchen. But how was that possible? She and the kids saw him, talked with him, hugged him.

"Don't bother coming to the hospital, Anna. You stay home with Mike and the kids. There's nothing to be done now. I'll come over later. I don't want to be alone on Thanksgiving . . . on the day your dad . . . I'm just so sorry you didn't get a chance to say goodbye to him."

Tears spilled from Anna's eyes.

But she and the children *had* said goodbye to him. She smiled through her tears. Somehow he made sure of that.

"Okay, Momma. We'll see you soon. And try not to be too sad. I know in my heart that Daddy went home on angel's wings."

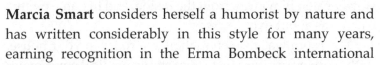

Marcia Smart considers herself a humorist by nature and has written considerably in this style for many years, earning recognition in the Erma Bombeck international writing contest.

She is also intrigued by psychological anomalies, crime-related drama and the unexplainable acts people commit against each other. Penning her first foray into the dark side, her book *Constant Killer* (available on Amazon) brings these elements together.

A retired interior redesigner, Marcia has authored DIY books, e-books, and training materials for the design industry.

Marcia lives in Southern California, where she is the organizer for the Conejo Valley Writers group and offers an editing service, www.EditingSmart.net.

DEATH

Alan Richard Zimmerman

The first time I encountered him—in person anyway—was about a year ago. I was sitting in a hospice bedroom waiting for my older brother, Bob, to die. For two years, cancer had slowly eaten him away from the inside, and his time on this earth was about over.

The room was nice enough, like a room in your house, with regular furniture instead of sterile medical equipment. Pictures of landscapes hung on the walls, but nothing personal. I brought a couple of my brother's old football trophies to make it seem more like home, but it didn't help me much, and I'm sure he never knew they were there. They even had a recliner that I slept in when weariness overcame my ability to keep up the vigil.

After years of surgery and chemotherapy, my brother's body was finally giving up, leaving him with nothing but horrible, unyielding pain. The nurses had already medicated him to the point of incoherence, so when the doctors said he had only days left, I decided to put him in hospice care. I hadn't counted on six days of waiting for the end. Each day brought a blessing and a curse: another day to spend with my brother, but also like a glimmer of hope for a miracle that wasn't going to come.

I spent the days talking to him, praying for him, singing to him, saying how much I loved him. I recounted every play of every football game I could remember. They say that hearing is the last thing to go (I don't know how anybody knows this), but I never even got the slightest reaction from him. I held his hand for hours, hoping for a twitch, a squeeze to let me know he was there, but nothing.

The last day seemed like the others. My brother just lay there in what was left of his world, oblivious to everything around him but the pain. You could only guess how he felt by the sound of his breathing. When it got louder or raspier, it was time for more morphine. The nurses delivered the doses on a schedule; they moved him around, bathed him, and treated him like he was still worth something.

I was telling Bob about the time he saved me from the neighborhood bully when it happened. I didn't notice at first, but I realized he had stopped breathing. He looked the same, but the rise and fall of his chest had stopped. I felt for a heartbeat or a pulse. He was gone. I leaned over him and told him—told myself, really—that I would see him again in heaven. I didn't cry like I thought I would; I guess I had spent enough tears the last twenty-four months and didn't have any left.

When I got up to get the nurse, I was shocked to see a man on the other side of the bed. He wore dark gray and black clothes, with a hooded shirt covering most of his head. He had a swarthy complexion and a small, sinister mouth. I shuddered when I saw his eyes: black and soulless, like looking into a void.

"How did you get in here?" I asked him.

The man smiled, which looked to me like a grimace, as his bony fingers reached out to touch my brother's arm. "He's mine now."

"Who are you? What do you think you're doing?"

He was staring at Bob like he was a prize, but then he looked up at me. "You know who I am. You know." And just like that, he disappeared.

It wasn't long until I saw him again. Bob's death had me thinking about my own mortality, and while I was jogging, I felt a slight tightness in my chest. I was sure it was tension and then I saw him sitting on a park bench.

"I'm waiting for you," he said.

The words sent a chill through my body. I knew who he was now. He had come for me, and I wasn't ready to go.

A couple of weeks later, in bed with the flu that had been going around, I couldn't stop thinking about the statistics of people dying from it and wondering if I would be one of those people. I had a fever, and after a fitful sleep, I woke covered in sweat. When I opened my eyes, I saw his face inches from mine. I could feel his hot breath on my cheeks.

"Are you ready for me?" he whispered.

I closed my eyes and felt my heart pounding in my chest, the veins pulsing in my neck, getting dizzy from hyperventilating. When I opened my eyes again, he had gone. I recovered from the flu but couldn't get away from the fear of my next appointment—maybe my final one—with Death.

For six months, I saw him everywhere: when I tripped on the stairs, when I had a close call in traffic, every ache and pain. I would look up, and there he was, taunting me to make sure I knew I was only one step, or misstep, away from the grave.

My life became a game of trying to avoid him. I avoided anything risky, doing everything I could to keep him at bay. My world closed in around me.

A few months ago, I had a strange dream—probably not so strange considering my preoccupation. In my dream, people were saying everything I had ever heard about death: "Death where is thy sting?" "Death and taxes." "If you eat it, you will surely die." "*Death of a Salesman.*" "I'll never get out of this world alive." "In the long run, we're all dead." "All that lives must die." "Will not die but have eternal life." The dream, which probably lasted a few seconds, seemed to go on for hours.

When I woke up, I felt unsettled. It didn't make any sense to me. When I walked outside to take my daily jog, I saw that it was overcast, threatening to rain. As I ran through the park, the heavy air weighed on my lungs, making me more tired than normal. I stopped to catch my breath, and I saw him on the park bench again.

"I'm here. I'm waiting for you," he said with his sick smile.

I don't know why, but this time I didn't run away. I walked over to the bench and sat beside him. He inched away from me, and his face turned into a sneer as I encroached on his territory.

"Why are you here? Why are you following me?" I asked him.

"You know why I'm here. I'm here for you."

I don't know where my courage came from, but I said, "Then take me. Right now."

"I'll take you when I'm ready!"

I shook my head slowly. "You can't, can you? You don't have the power of life and death."

He held out his evil finger and pointed it at me. "If I touch you, you will die. You will be mine."

Somehow I knew he was lying, so I reached out and grabbed his hand. Nothing happened. He pulled away and his face turned even uglier.

"You have no power over me," I told him. "None at all."

He stared at me for a moment and then stiffened in defiance. "I have the power of suffering. Look at Bob, your wonderful brother. Suffering for years. What did he do to deserve that? Nothing. I made him suffer."

"No. I don't know why he suffered. He didn't take care of himself. He smoked. He drank too much. Maybe he caused his own suffering. Maybe it was because of how he treated his ex-wife. Maybe it wasn't even him. Maybe it was the sin of Adam. Maybe it's because the whole world is screwed up. But it wasn't you. You can't do anything."

He didn't even argue my point but tried another approach. "I have the power of fear. You're proof of that. And fear is even worse than death."

"You only have that power if I give it to you."

He smirked at me. "What are you saying? That you aren't afraid to die?"

"I know I'm going to die. Everybody is going to die. We can't stop it. Why would I fear something that's inevitable? What I'm really afraid of is not living."

"That's the same thing, you know."

I shook my head again. "Dying? I can't control that. But living? That I can do. And you can't stop me."

He just looked at me, his anger replaced by indifference.

"Why are you even here? What do you really do?" I asked him.

"I wait. I wait for people to die. Then I take their bodies—and most of their souls."

"Most of their souls?"

"That's what I said. Some of them I can't have."

"Like mine?"

He didn't answer but got up and walked away.

~~~

I own a gift shop at Santa Barbara Harbor. People come in and buy trinkets to remind themselves and their friends that they visited the Pacific Ocean. They are usually as pleasant as the weather and have plenty of spending money. I was finishing with a customer when an odd-looking man in a white linen suit and a panama hat walked in.

"Good morning," I greeted him. "Can I help you?"

The man just looked around the store as he approached the counter.

I tried again. "Can I show you something?"

"Don't you remember me?" the man said.

I surely would have remembered a strange character like that, so I gave him a second look. That's when I noticed his eyes: black and soulless.

"Death?" I asked.

"Don't worry." He smiled. "I'm not here for you."

I hadn't thought about him in months and really didn't know what to say.

"I hardly recognized you. You certainly have changed."

He shook his head. "No, I haven't changed at all. You just see me differently."

Our meeting was awkward and uncomfortable. We know each other, but we're not friends.

"Nice store you have here," he said, "but I need to be going. I have a busy day. Lots of appointments, you know."

I nodded, then asked a question just to hear what he would say.

"When am I going to see you again?"

He lifted his hands in an apologetic gesture and said, "God only knows."

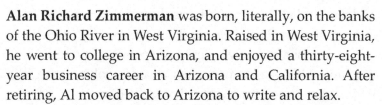

Alan Richard Zimmerman was born, literally, on the banks of the Ohio River in West Virginia. Raised in West Virginia, he went to college in Arizona, and enjoyed a thirty-eight-year business career in Arizona and California. After retiring, Al moved back to Arizona to write and relax.

He has written and self-published novels, poetry, self-help works, short stories, comedy pieces, cartoons, and music.

To learn more, visit his website, www.ideajuicer.net.

RETURN TO SENDER

Deborah Brawders

––––––––––◦◈◈◦––––––––––

The stifling heat in the train pulled Eliot out of his seat. As his station rolled into view, he pushed through the sea of passengers, stepping out into the cool air. A slight unevenness under his foot caused him to look down. A once bright red envelope lay under his shoe, sullied by a parade of hurried feet. Someone had scratched through the address and written in dark, bold letters:

RETURN TO SENDER

Those words smacked of rejection.

Eliot had never received a valentine. In his mind, it was a foolish celebration pushed by the florists, chocolatiers, and restaurants. Still, for a moment, he felt a pang of loss. At forty, he had once again launched an unsuccessful foray into cyberdating, where love proved to be as elusive and mercurial as ever.

He glanced up as the next train lurched along the platform, its windows fogged with the impatient breath of commuters. Curiosity drove Eliot to grasp the envelope just as the train screeched to a stop. A rush of passengers carried him up the stairs and out onto the pavement.

He glanced at the sender's address: 14 Bluebird Lane, London WC1.

It was only a street away.

Eliot hesitated.

No good could come from this, yet he felt strangely compelled to return it to the sender.

A letter box beckoned as Eliot walked into Bluebird Lane. His fingers tightened against the envelope while his mind railed at the foolishness of his mission.

He stopped outside number fourteen. Had fate sent him so hope wouldn't linger on Bluebird Lane?

His fingers loosened against the red burden, and he turned to leave.

The door opened.

Cornflower blue eyes, soft brown curls, and full lips held his stare.

"Er . . . sorry, I found this." He thrust the envelope toward her.

A frown cast a long shadow across her face.

"I live around the corner," he babbled. "Just thought I should . . ."

"My sister. I told her it was a waste of time."

The soft lilt of her accent left Eliot wanting more.

"Unrequited love," she explained, then added, "I know you. You're always on the 7:15 train, studying your *Financial Times* in the fourth carriage, second seat from the end."

Eliot's mouth opened and closed, willing his brain to give some response, but it had shut down in a cloud of conflicting emotions. Finally, he extracted himself, mumbling something as he retreated down the path. His hurried footsteps led him home, but all the while, he picked away at her words.

She had observed him and he had been oblivious. Safely tucked into his newspaper and absorbed by world events, he had missed something much closer to home.

Something important.

Roused by his 6:15 alarm, Eliot started his well-trodden routine. A cup of coffee, lightened with just a splash of milk; a slice and a half of whole wheat bread, toasted only on one side. Picking up his newspaper from the doormat, he noted the date.

February fourteenth.

That other traveler with a penchant for the fourth carriage on the 7:15 pricked at his thoughts.

He boarded the train and buried himself in an article on the front page of the *Financial Times*. It wasn't long before his eyes and thoughts wandered.

He glanced over the paper.

In the fourth seat from the end, he caught cornflower blue eyes, soft brown curls, and a ghost of a smile on full red lips.

Perhaps a valentine lay in his future, courtesy of "return to sender."

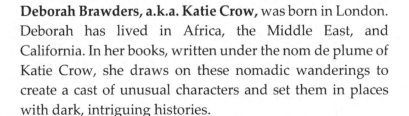

Deborah Brawders, a.k.a. Katie Crow, was born in London. Deborah has lived in Africa, the Middle East, and California. In her books, written under the nom de plume of Katie Crow, she draws on these nomadic wanderings to create a cast of unusual characters and set them in places with dark, intriguing histories.

Most days you can find Deborah hiking, gardening, or running plot ideas past her trusty companion, a rescued terrier named Winston.

To learn more about Deborah's books, visit her author website, https://katiecrow.com/.

APRIL FOOLS

Alex Holub

———————◦◇◦———————

Justin races to the kitchen when he hears his mother walk in. "Did you get them, Mom? Did you?"

His mother places two bags of groceries on the kitchen counter. "Yes, Justin. I got them."

Justin rummages through the bags and pulls out the items he wants. "Super cool, Mom. Thanks."

"You're welcome," his mother says. "Although I don't know why you wanted . . ." She's interrupted by her phone. "Hi Patsy, yes, we're still on." Her voice trails off as she walks into the living room.

Justin scrolls through Pinterest, finds the caramel apple recipe he wants, and goes to work. Thirty minutes later, he's placing the finished items, wrapped in colored tissue paper, into a white box.

"Okay, Mom, I'm finished," Justin yells. "The kitchen's yours. I'm going over to Charlie's."

"Be back in time for supper."

"I will." Holding the box, he jumps on his bike and heads for Charlie's house.

Charlie's changing the chain on his bike when Justin rides up. "Are they finished?"

"Right here." Justin pats the box he's holding.

Charlie takes the box, looks inside, and sees twelve wrapped items. "Which ones are which?"

"I don't know."

"Oh, great." Charlie hands the box back and finishes tightening the chain.

Justin studies the box. It looks naked. "Do you think we should write something?"

Charlie's picking up his tools. "Like what?"

"I don't know. Maybe something like—Hands off! This means you!"

Charlie tosses the tools into his toolbox. "How about something a little softer? Like, FREE Caramel Apples."

"I like it. I like it a lot," says Justin. "Do you have a marker?"

~~~

The following morning, Justin and Charlie arrive at school a half hour early and head for the teachers' lounge. As Justin had hoped, it's empty.

"Keep watch while I put the box in the fridge," says Justin. He's closing the door when Charlie whistles. Justin races from the lounge seconds before Butch "Hard-Ass" Blackburn and Taylor "No-Neck" Wilson, the two most disliked teachers in the school, enter.

Justin and Charlie walk a short way down the hall, make a sharp U-turn, and head back to the lounge. They stop next to the door and peer around the edge.

No Neck drops his briefcase on the table and opens the fridge. "Hey, Butch, look at this," he says, lifting out the white box.

"What's that?"

"It looks like somebody left a box of free caramel apples."

"Well, open it and see."

No-Neck opens the box and sees twelve round objects with protruding wooden sticks. "Yep, caramel apples, all right."

"Better be careful," says Butch. "Remember, it's April first. You don't want to be the butt of an April Fools' joke, do you?"

"No, but they sure look good." Reluctantly, No-Neck picks up the box and walks toward the refrigerator.

Justin's face drops, then brightens when No-Neck says, "Aw heck, I'm willing to take the chance." He opens the box, takes out an apple, removes the tissue paper, and bites into the crunchy caramel coating. When No-Neck finishes chewing, he says, "Hmmm, delicious. So much for an April fools' joke. You should try one."

Hard-Ass is tempted but not convinced. He hesitates before the mouthwatering aroma of caramel overcomes his better judgment. He grabs an apple, chomps down . . . and bellowing like a constipated moose, races to the sink.

No-Neck jumps up. "What's wrong?"

Hard-Ass's mouth is under the faucet, spitting out chunks of caramel onion.

"Gotcha," Justin whispers. "April fool."

Hard-Ass sputters, "If I catch the SOB who did that, I'll nail his hide to the wall."

No-Neck drapes his arm over his friend's shoulder and says, "Calm down. Maybe we can have some fun with this."

"With whom?"

"Our peers. What if we leave the box on the table and let them decide if they want an apple."

A devious smile crosses Hard-Ass's lips as he and No-Neck sit down to wait for their first victim.

~~~

"May I help you, young gentlemen?"

Justin spins around and comes nose-to-drooping bust with Ms. Marion C. Butterworth, the school's principal. Students refer to her as Butter Butt.

"N-no, Ms. Butt . . . erworth. We were on our way to class when we heard Mr. Blackburn yell, so we stopped to see if we could help."

"Very commendable," says the principal, looking into the lounge. "But everything seems to be under control. You'd better hurry, or you'll be late for class."

"Yes, ma'am," Justin and Charlie answer in unison. They start to leave, but Justin looks back and sees Ms. Butterworth disappear into the lounge. It's an opportunity too tempting to pass up. He backpedals to the door and peeks in. Butter Butt is pointing to the box. Hard-Ass and No-Neck shake their heads and shrug their shoulders. Ms. Butterworth opens the box and lifts an object wrapped in purple tissue paper. Justin hears her say, "I'll save it for lunch. If you find out who left them, say thank you for me."

Justin and Charlie's morning classes pass quickly. They feel home free until lunch, when they hear their names over the loudspeaker: "Justin Fredericks and Charlie Carlson report to the principal's office." There's no please or thank you.

"Uh-oh," Charlie says, staring at Justin, who's biting into a cheeseburger. "You don't think someone squealed, do you?"

Justin swallows and says, "Who'd squeal? We're the only ones who know what's in the box."

Justin and Charlie are ushered into Ms. Butterworth's office five minutes later. Sitting on her desk in plain sight is an April fools' apple. Ms. Butterworth points to the apple with fire in her eyes. "What do you two know about that?"

"It looks like a caramel apple," says Justin.

"Look closer."

He does and sees a sizable chunk missing, revealing the skin of an onion. "Why would we know anything about that?"

"Because I caught you two peeking into the teacher's lounge right after Mr. Blackburn let out that blood-curdling shriek."

"We plead the Fifth," Justin says.

"Fair enough. Then I'm going to suspend you both for a week."

Tears form at the corners of Charlie's eyes. "Is-is there a second option?"

"Actually, there is," Ms. Butterworth says. "You can sample what's in this box."

Justin stares at the bold black letters: FREE Caramel Apples. "Can Charlie and I have a couple of minutes in private?"

"I don't see why not," Ms. Butterworth says as she struggles out of her chair and shuffles from the office.

Justin slumps down. "Damn and double damn."

"How many April Fools' apples did you make?" says Charlie.

"Two. Why?"

"I'm not sure, but if we count the one No-Neck bit into, it means there's only one left, and there are ten apples in the box."

"Meaning what?"

"We have a 10 percent chance of getting a caramel onion. It's better than getting suspended."

"I'm not so sure. Have you ever bitten into an onion?"

Ms. Butterworth reenters the room with Hard-Ass and No-Neck close behind. "Well, have you decided?"

Justin looks at the two new arrivals. "How many weeks' detention?"

"I said one, but Mr. Blackburn thinks it should be two."

Charlie grabs his heart. "Two weeks' detention! My father will kill me. I vote for the apple tasting."

Ms. Butterworth steeples her chubby fingers and stares at Justin. He doesn't have the same worry as Charlie, but knows he'll be grounded for a month.

"Well, Justin?" Hard-Ass says. "What's it going to be? Suspension or the apples?"

"Can I have more time to decide?"

"No," Ms. Butterworth snaps. "You have one minute to make up your mind. Then I'm going to suspend you."

Onion breath or detention? Neither seems appealing. What Justin had been looking forward to all year is ending up biting him in the ass.

Ms. Butterworth looks at her phone. "Thirty seconds."

"Alright, alright. I'll taste the darn apples."

Ms. Butterworth opens the box. "Good choice. Who wants to go first?"

"I have a better idea," Hard-Ass says. "Let's have them both sample an apple on the count of three."

Sweat breaks out on Charlie and Justin's foreheads as they reach for the tissue-wrapped apples. Justin chooses red, Charlie green. They unwrap the apples and wait for the countdown to begin.

"One . . . two . . . three . . . bite."

Justin and Charlie chomp down.

Ms. Butterworth, No-Neck, and Hard-Ass wait.

At first, there's nothing. Then, like an erupting volcano, Justin and Charlie explode from their seats, spitting out chunks of onion as they bolt for the water fountains.

Justin's gulping down water when he hears Hard-Ass, No-Neck, and Ms. Butterworth laughing and shouting, "April fools'!"

Justin's brow is furrowed with confusion when he returns to his chair. "But-but there should only have been one April Fools' apple left."

"So, you admit you left the apples," Ms. Butterworth says.

"Yeah," Justin mutters. "It was my idea. Charlie just went along for the ride. But why did—?"

Ms. Butterworth finishes the question. "—you both get onions? Because I had the cooks in the cafeteria replace all the apples with onions."

Alex Holub is a corporate executive, long-time business owner, and full-time fiction writer since retiring five years ago. His short stories run the genre gamut from children's to humor to horror—all with twist endings.

He is working on a novel featuring an offbeat independent contractor (detective) whose business card reads: WHATEVER IT TAKES.

Alex lives with his wife and two cats in Moorpark, California.

ELDERS OF BAYVIEW

Hal T. Horowitz

———————◦◇◇◦———————

Mythomaniac: Someone who cannot tell the difference between truth and falsehood. In other words, one who doesn't know whether he's lying or telling the truth.

Cal negotiated his Indian motorcycle over the compacted snow, past the "Welcome to Bayview" sign. He passed a fenced-in gravel pit, an arrow pointing up a narrow dirt access to a sawmill, and a parking lot occupied by some dump trucks and yellow earthmovers. About half a mile beyond, a small, unlit library and a few small shops— appliance repair, antiques, and the like—all closed, announced the outskirts of the town. *Where's the bay?*

Seeing lights flickering on ahead of him along the one-road town, Cal took his sunglasses from his forehead and dropped them into the breast pocket of his fleece-lined leather jacket. It was a good jacket, but with the solstice nearing, it could barely keep him from shivering. *Somewhere along this desolate road there had to be a restaurant. Food. More importantly, warmth. And most importantly, a phone.* His temples throbbed. *I need to find a phone.*

He found it sooner than he'd expected: Maye's Diner. The lights were on, people were inside, and its flashing neon sign gave it an air of near levity. He skidded his bike onto the snowy gravel and drove up to an old, splintered hitching rail standing over the rotted foundation of some since used trough. Stepping onto the porch, Cal brushed a few flakes of new powdered snow off his sleeve.

"How do, young fella. Can we help ya?" The speaker had short white hair, a thin mustache, and ice-blue eyes.

Cal scanned the room. Seven men sat around two tables, all seemingly frozen in mid-conversation, with their eyes now on him. Farthest from the door, the speaker stood, allowing his tweed jacket to hang open.

"Yes sir." Cal eyed him, then the remainder of the septet. His voice turned awkwardly breathy. "I need a phone. I can't get a signal here. I just saw a man get shot. Killed." His still cold lungs slowed his drawl. "Back up on the road. Where's your phone?"

"What kind of signal?" asked another from the same table, a shaggy-haired man in a blue turtleneck.

"Yes, what signal?" It was a voice from the other table.

"A wireless signal." He held up his phone.

"Oh, one of those kind o' signals. Well, that won't work out here, son. Why do you need it?"

"Well, to call the police, sir. I told you I just saw a man get shot." *Are these people all stupid?*

"Dead? You saw a man get shot dead?" the silver-haired man in the tweed asked.

"Yes sir."

"I witnessed a man get shot dead once," a man from the second table spoke up. Cal looked at him. He had a high, pronounced forehead, a noticeable overbite, and wore old fashion wire-framed glasses. "They done got the son of a bitch that did it, too. Put him away on my testimony, they did. Think it's the same guy?"

Cal looked at him. "I wouldn't know, sir."

"Well, who is it ya say got shot, son?"

"I wouldn't know that either, mister. I'm not from around here."

"When'd this supposed killing happen?" The man in tweed asked.

"Maybe forty, fifty minutes ago. And it wasn't a 'supposed killing.' I witnessed it and I gotta call the police to report it. Now."

"Well, first of all, young man," a rotund and jowly looking man slurred from the first table, "we don't have any police around here. Just a county sheriff. And second, I don't 'spect he'll believe you."

"Won't believe me? Why wouldn't he believe me? I can show him."

One of the group members issued a low chuckle, just loud enough to be heard and become mildly contagious.

Cal went on, "I was coming north on my bike on the county highway, about twelve, thirteen miles back. Wasn't goin' too fast 'cause the road was slick from the snow, when suddenly some guy in an old station wagon goes speedin' by . . ."

"Old station wagon?" the shaggy guy asked. "That'd be Sam Carver."

"Yeah," another voice chimed in from under a fedora. "Say, who did Sam kill?"

"He didn't kill anyone. He was being chased by another guy. He's the guy who got killed."

"Well, which 'he' are ya referrin' to?"

"The 'he' that was being chased got killed by the 'he' that was chasing him."

"Well, he probably had it coming, you know," the man with the fedora said. "He was a nasty son of a bitch. How'd he get him? Did he shoot from the moving car?"

"No. This Sam guy, he lost control and slid off the highway into a snowbank. I was goin' to head my bike over there when I saw the second fella stop and get out with a gun. He just walked over, opened Sam's door, and shot him. Just shot him! Then Sam, if that's who you say it was, he just leaned halfway out the door, and the killer sloshed back to his car and left. After he was out of sight, I went over to check on this guy Sam, and he's just lying there with blood comin' through his jacket and all. He was dead, sure enough. I'll take the sheriff out there and show him."

"And what makes ya think the sheriff will believe it weren't you who shot him?" It was a new voice from the second table, a stocky, full-bearded man in a green flannel shirt and plaid hunting cap.

"That's just crazy. I didn't kill him." He pulled his phone out of his pocket and checked. Still no service bars. "Come on," he pleaded. "We gotta get the sheriff out here. That killer could be miles away by now."

"Or he could be standin' right here, young fella," the man insisted.

"That's ridiculous, mister! I didn't shoot no one. Hell, I don't even own a gun."

"I own a gun. Three of them," the bucktoothed man with the wire-framed specs offered.

"Now, no you don't, Harvey." The gentleman in tweed stood up to argue with him. "Don't go saying stupid things like that. You know you don't own three guns. Just an old Remington shotgun."

"I do so own three guns, Walter. I'm the sheriff here, aren't I? I need three guns."

"No. We have a sheriff, Harvey, but it ain't you." The response came from a meek-looking but booming-voiced man at Harvey's table."

"Sit down and shut up, George. Why're ya spreadin' lies? Ya know I'm the sheriff here. Well, the deputy, anyhow."

"You ain't anymore, Harvey, and you don't own three guns. Now tell the boy here the truth."

"Ain't we all tellin' him the truth, Walter?"

"Gentlemen, I don't know what's going on here, and honestly, I don't care. I just want to call the sheriff, whoever he is. Now, are you his deputy?"

"I am."

"He ain't."

"I am."

"You ain't, Harvey." A waitress came out from the kitchen with a tray of pie slices. "You know you're not the deputy any longer, Harvey. Now sit down and eat your pie." She set a plate in front of him.

Everyone laughed.

"Sit down, young man," the waitress instructed Cal. "Have a piece of pie."

"Thank you, ma'am, but I just need to make a call. Where's the phone?"

"He wants t' call the sheriff, Maye," the man with the white hair and thin mustache said. "Says he witnessed Sam Carver get killed."

"That's ridiculous. Sam called his dinner order in not half an hour ago."

"Are you all crazy?" Cal tried to shout above the din. "I don't know if it was this Sam Carver or if it was John Doe who got shot, but I know what I saw. Now isn't anyone here going to tell me where there's a phone? There's a dead man out there. Don't you all care? You, sir?" Cal addressed the one man who hadn't spoken yet. He wore a clerical collar.

"Gentlemen!" The cleric was calm, with a deep, resonating voice. "This boy here's sayin' he just seen someone shot and killed, and the murderer is probably up to the next town by now. We got to stop messin' with him now and get hold of the sheriff."

Cal took a breath. "Thank you, reverend."

"Oh, he ain't no reverend," Harvey said. "No more a reverend than I'm the sheriff."

"So what if he's not?" Cal asked. "He just told you we got to get the sheriff out here."

"He is too a reverend," the meek-looking man's voice boomed.

"Then I'm the sheriff."

"Shut up, Harvey. You ain't no sheriff and you don't own three guns and you never saw no one get killed."

Cal turned to look from man to man, from voice to voice. *Are they all nuts?*

A sudden chill blew in, drawing everyone's attention to the door before it slammed shut, demanding immediate silence. A tall man with broad shoulders, wearing a khaki military-style uniform adorned by a bright silver star on his chest, stomped a bit of snow off his boots and stood beneath the overhead entry light. "Hi, boys." His voice was deep and intense. "What's going on in here? Who's this young gent?" He pointed at Cal. "That your 'cycle sitting outside?"

"Yes. Are you the sheriff here, sir?"

"I am. These fellows been entertaining you with their lies?"

"Lies?" Cal asked. "I've been trying to tell them to call you. I saw a man get shot and killed back up on the road a while ago."

"Who was that?"

"I wouldn't know."

Cal noticed a sudden quiet in the diner. *Finally.*

"Was about an hour ago. I saw a red car chasing a gray station wagon. When the wagon hit a snowbank, the guy chasing it got out of the car and shot the driver. Killed him, sheriff. I stopped to see if I could help."

"Help the man who was shot?"

"Yes, but he was already dead."

"Did you get a license number of the red car?"

"No."

"Can you tell me what the driver looked like? What he was wearing?"

"No. He had an overcoat and a hat, and he had a scarf over his face."

"For someone who wants to help, you're not doing a good job."

The diner door opened again, then slammed shut. Cal's eyes widened in sudden horror. "You!"

A man, blood dripping from his shirt, stumbled in and slumped into a booth near the door.

"Sam, what the hell happened?" the reverend asked.

"I'll tell you what happened, Ralph. This jackass here," he pointed to the sheriff, "left me lying in the snow freezin' my ass off after he shot me. The blood's from the crash. Then—" He looked at Cal. "Who're you?"

"I'm Cal. I stopped to help you."

"Oh, right. Then 'Cal' here, he stops, touches me, and says, 'Oh shit,' and runs off. Big help you were."

"Sorry, sir. I thought you were dead."

"Well, I might have been, no thanks to you." Sam cracked some of the frozen blood from his jacket.

"So, what do ya' think we should do?" the sheriff asked.

"I'll tell you what we should do," Sam said, still playing with the blood on his jacket. "Next time, let the reverend here be the sheriff. You can be the one who gets killed out there and I'll just sit back here where it's nice and warm."

No one noticed Cal leave. The Indian sputtered a bit as it started, its rear wheel skidding slightly as he pulled away from the hitching post, the trough base, and the two cars now parked on either side of him, one a red sedan and the other an old, gray, dented station wagon.

Where's the bay?

Hal T. Horowitz began making up tales at age twelve. They were often humorous and usually centered around his family, for his cousin's Sunday school class. By high school, he was writing them as short stories.

Hal was born in Chicago and came to Los Angeles with his parents in 1954 at age ten. He was a business administration major and peppered his studies with courses in journalism, art, and creative writing. Hal returned to college after his discharge from the air force in 1963. He had a thirty-two-year career in commercial finance and equipment leasing, followed by a second career of twenty-two years as a bank recruiter, career counselor, and EQ mentor, during all of which he continued to try to improve his writing craft.

He has written numerous business articles for a variety of trade newspapers and magazines, and has had his short story *The Cemetery Picnics* selected for publication as an "Outstanding Writing" in the 1997 California Writers Club, San Fernando Valley anthology, *Down in the Valley*. He has also written and contributed to numerous plays and skits for private organizations and groups.

Now retired, Hal is devoting his full attention to caring for his wife, Barbara, and writing. He is optimistic about seeing his most recent work, a five-generation family saga titled *Forward tho' I cannot see*, published by the end of 2023.

THE THOUSAND STEPS

Jeanne Rawlings

---◇◈◇---

The sun set behind the hospital earlier every day, which made his task a bit harder. After all, it was almost *el Día de los Muertos*, Julio thought, kissing his medallion and crossing himself. Turning on his flashlight, he watched his shadow simply disappear into the black hole overhead.

Wearing green scrubs, he crawled from the ladder into the hospital ductwork like a beetle. It was his job to clean the rat bait stations, a task no one wanted. He was last on the seniority list, and besides, he was very small. But these days he was remarkably willing. Unusually so.

"*Uno, dos, tres.*" He counted each step on hands and knees, mapping the twists and turns of the long metal tubes. He'd gone far beyond where he was supposed to be.

In Room 556, Anna lay in the semidarkness. Her TV muted, she watched the orange sky turn to black. The nurses passed her door, wheeling carts with dinners, but she was always last. Putting on and taking off protective gear for just one isolation patient was a nuisance.

A familiar voice rang out, "Four hundred ninety-nine!"

A tile slid back, and Julio gazed down from the ceiling above the door. "*Quinientos!* Five hundred steps!" Their eyes met, his laughing and hers filling with tears. It was their game, these weeks she'd been so sick.

He never came down. Couldn't manage it, really. But he'd visited faithfully ever since she arrived, even bringing flowers and tossing them onto her bed.

"Take me up with you tonight," she whispered. "I can make the thousand-step journey."

"Ah, my *conejita*, my bunny, how can you? You cannot fly. And you will not fit."

She lifted her arms to him and again said in her broken English, "I will crawl with you."

"You will walk," he soothed her, "but through the hallway. And not crawling . . . when you are strong."

Julio talked about Thanksgiving, then. That she'd be home, certainly. And tonight—the family making food for the ancestors' graves on *el Día de los Muertos*.

Suddenly, the door swung open and silenced them. A tall nurse, fully gowned from head to toe, shoved a meal cart into the room. Whisps of bright red hair poked out from under her scrub cap.

"A light dinner only, tonight, hon. No cookie."

As the nurse prattled on with her back to him, Julio closed up the ceiling gently. Minutes ticked by, and then he heard nothing. Unable to contain himself, he dared to peek down. Anna was gone. Stunned, his eyes darted around the room. Everything was there: The flowers he'd brought, in vases all around. The window, black with night. Except his *espousa*, his wife, was gone.

Helpless and desperate to find her, he began crawling back. Sweat dripped onto the floor beneath his hands. Shaking, the flashlight beam flitted every which way, and dizziness turned his stomach.

"Five hundred twenty. Or is it six twenty?" he asked. The turns he made by measuring steps eluded him. It's a maze, he thought. Or a tomb.

The faint sounds from the rooms below calmed him. Switching off the light, he let the natural dimness draw his gaze. There, only yards away, was the opening to the ladder and escape. He began crawling again, until Anna's voice stopped him.

"A thousand steps home . . . coming with you."

"Anna?" he choked out.

"My daughter will be home tonight."

A chill froze him in place. *Mi suegra!* He was certain beyond a doubt that the voice was his mother-in-law. She had passed years ago.

"*Suegra!* Please!" he whispered. A shadow covered the opening as though a door had shut. He was in total darkness. Clasping his holy pendant, he began to pray. "Mother, have mercy."

The medallion moved in his palm. Emboldened, Julio prayed on.

"Hey," a small voice called from below.

The dark tunnel lit up. Someone was shining a light through the access.

"*Si!* Yes!" Julio shouted. Whoever it was, he could see now. In seconds he was plunging his legs through to the ladder.

"*Si!* It's Julio Gonzales! On the job!" But when his head cleared the opening, he saw only an empty room.

"Hello?" he whispered, as ice crept up his back and lifted the hairs on his neck. It made no sense, and yet everything seemed senseless now. All that mattered was to find Anna.

Making his way to the trash room, he donned a face mask, gloves, and a hood. He reappeared in the hall behind a large waste container, like an ant pushing a huge load.

At the ICU wing, he hovered. Would his badge give him access? Before he could try, the double doors opened. A nurse exited and smiled. He politely let her pass and caught the door before it could shut. When she was out of sight, he ditched the trash bin against a wall.

Inside, the unfamiliar hallway slowed him down. A numbness began to fill him. He floated past the nurses' station like a ghost, and no one looked up. If they did, what did it matter? If his beloved was gone, what did anything matter?

With no sense of direction, he began to wander.

The red-haired nurse coming from Room 556 drew him like a beacon. As he approached, she eyed his badge, and he dimly realized he didn't have a single piece of cleaning gear with him.

"Kinda late," she quipped. "I thought they were sending teams now, to sanitize iso rooms." Her voice was tired.

He stood staring at the closed door. The nurse was walking away. What was he waiting for? Permission to enter? On this eve of *el Día de los Muertos*, with the medallion burning against his chest, Julio managed to touch the doorknob but his fingers were frozen. It was the nurse who freed them with four words: "Patient's back. From radiology."

When he pushed open the door, a vision flooded him with relief.

"Mi amor," Anna said from the bed. She was alive. Until then, he hadn't realized how many flowers he'd brought her. From this angle, they seemed to fill the room.

"No more steps to count," Julio sang quietly into her ear as he held her close.

"No?" she answered. "No more thousand steps?"

"No more," he whispered.

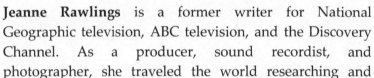

Jeanne Rawlings is a former writer for National Geographic television, ABC television, and the Discovery Channel. As a producer, sound recordist, and photographer, she traveled the world researching and writing many documentary films. She was nominated for five Emmy Awards, won two Emmys, and received dozens of national film awards before retiring.

Jeanne grew up in Maryland and received her bachelor's degree in English from Frostburg State University. She went on to write short stories, published nonfiction magazine articles, and edited several published memoirs, as well as an art history book.

Blog: https://www.mywisdomroad.com/

THE GIFT OF POETRY

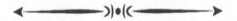

UNTITLED

Barbara Champlin

you are bay and shore
Golden Gate and Grant Avenue,
stained glass,
brick and brass,
clanging cable cars and
misty eucalyptus-scented nights.
your electric lights
jewel the horizon into
Stars.
you are people . . .
skin varied as silk
shaded mocha to saffron,
ivory to ebony,
as natural an array as the
carts of flowers on corners.
you are houses . . .
each house not even elbow room apart
race like rabbits on
perpendicular hills.

in your city I hold hands
with Strangers,
each face and hand
familiar as black coffee
and rain beating on
bay windows.

SUPREME COURT BLUES

Barbara Champlin

Oh, how we miss you, Mrs. Ginsburg
You left us way too soon
We still need you, Mrs. Ginsburg
And your bulldog bite on rights
Making humans equals
And free to make our choice
Your stratospheric intellect
And dead center rational
Was our compass in the chaos
The truth we steered toward
Please stay with us, Mrs. Ginsburg
Whisper in our ears
The better world we can create
One that will endure

Barbara Champlin started writing poetry from an early age when she discovered that poetry, using just a few well-chosen words, could tell an entire story, emotion, or opinion more profoundly than prose. It is a form of expression that she finds both a challenge and a pleasure.

Ms. Champlin also writes a travel blog whose sponsors include Collette Tours and Viking Cruises. www.TheWorldAccordingToBarbara.com

A TRIBUTE TO LOVE

Jamie Diep

This is a dedication to those who have lost their loved ones. May we all find comfort in our Lord Jesus Christ. God is the Way, the Truth, and the Light. He is our Savior.

A small and sad gal walked slowly home.
Home to an emptiness. No one here anymore,
She cried out to the universe.
Why had her love left without saying goodbye.
Thirty years plus. Now a giant VOID.
Their love was nice and sweet, not tumultuous.
There are times when life dealt them some hardships.
But through it all, they worked it out.
Communication was their practice.
Never go to bed angry.
She reflected on the good times and bad times.
But cannot understand why her man just up and left.
No explanations. Why is life so hard that he could not
    take it anymore.
Is life an illusion?
What is love that leaves you so totally broken?
He was her hero, her post, her everything.

He put her on her pedestal, treasured her.
She was always able to count on her man.
So proud to have such a solid and strong relationship.
They work side by side. Told her to count on him always.
Now, she's lost, broken and completely alone.
A few friends of hers told her to hate him and move on.
She resented such suggestions.
All she had was love and gratefulness to him.
So full of many wonderful memories.
But as she grieves for such loss.
Thinking is that all to life?
She thanked God for sustaining her.
HE is forever faithful.
HE had sent angels to comfort her.
As she's struggling to overcome her grief.
Slowly, she gained her strength, her confidence, she lost her fear.
Hallelujah, God be praised.
Now it has been over five years and six months since he left her world.
She is continuing on knowing Life is beautiful.
Thinking of him, knowing she will see him again.
Seeing two souls will dance for eternity again.
Until then, she is moving on.

WHAT IS LIFE?

Jamie Diep

Life is a blessing, a journey of self-discovery.
Life is full of twists and turns.
It can be Ces't la Vie or Ces't la Guerre.
Life is full of ups and downs, peaks and valleys.
Life can be viewed as a glass half full or half empty.
With the right frame of mind, positive outlook,
it can propel us to the right destination.
If human beings are able to understand and appreciate
    what we have been given:
A gift of life, freedom to choose, born in a good family,
    being raised by good parenting,
to live in a democratic country, able to pursue an
    education, freedom to express ourselves,
and receive abundant blessings, things we see, things
    we don't see.
Through challenges, we learn to be grateful, thankful
    and humble,
as we struggle to overcome all of life difficulties.
All life is precious.
Each moment is a memory to treasure.
Love one another.
Let's make this a better world for everyone.

Love is the energy that binds our lives.
Pass this forward. It starts with us.

———————◦◆◇◆◦———————

Jamie Diep was born in Danang, Vietnam, in 1959. She emigrated to America with her family in 1975. They were among the first Vietnamese refugees to escape the conflict and be sent for processing to Camp Pendleton in California.

She graduated from Hollywood High School in 1979 and later enrolled in UCLA. In her third year, Jamie left school to run multiple family businesses. She was married to Anthony Cardoza for thirty-three years, but lost him in 2015 due to ill health. During the COVID-19 pandemic and quarantine, she found time for art and writing.

She is working on a biography detailing her family's struggle in Vietnam, and hopes to become a documentary writer.

SONNETS FOR MY BELOVED A

Michael Edelstein

Hello my one and only Dear
You fill my heart with lambent cheer
We've been together less this year
My hours are greener when you're near
My hopes for us are filled with charms
Replete as with you in my arms
Your words are my much needed balms
Your song causes my storm to calm
My mind is tossed as if by sea
I find no warmth that fosters me
Days are shadows as hours flee
I wish that we as one might be
My skin is lonely for your touch
I want you with me evermuch

SONNETS FOR MY BELOVED B

Michael Edelstein

O'er time, we've all Medusa's face
There's no art we cannot debase
Polymaths all elude disgrace
Our truths I fear are all mistakes
My fire for you will always burn
My spirit's trapped now in a churn
I pray that you'll disclaim your spurn
For our oneness I dearly yearn
Through vacant worlds we leave no trace
Humankind thrives in contumace
We're naught but atoms in one place
Pray grant me life in your embrace
Time is void when we are alone
Let's be forever two as one

Dr. Michael Edelstein, MD, MBA, practiced medicine from 1962 through 2015. He has written and read poetry for as long as he can remember.

He was Brooklyn JHS 149's 1950 poet laureate, and still has the medal to show for it. Dr. Edelstein has retired to a career in writing, especially as a poet, and is working on a prose-poetry memoir, *A Doctor's Journey through Strokeland.*

APPROACHING 80

Bonnie Goldenberg

Having survived what John Updike called
the decade in which most people die,
including him at 77,
I now face the surreal next one,
the one in which I will most likely
disappear, too.
The reality is both frightening,
and also kind of lonely,
because unlike the huge numbers of
baby boomers born
after the men came home from
the war in '46,
those of us who arrived
during those terrible war years,
are a much smaller cohort.
I can imagine it now —
the volumes of memoir,
poetry, stories, articles
about what it feels like
to be where I am now
that they will write.
How they will be more

able to comfort each other,
ease the transition to whatever
they believe comes next.
To say I'm not even close
to dealing with this
is an understatement,
even though I know
I am lucky to have survived
until now
thanks to modern medicine,
a middle-class lifestyle
that has allowed me to enjoy
a comfortable place to live,
and plentiful good food,
denied to so many
both here and worldwide.
On her deathbed,
my mother, who passed at 86
from sudden onset leukemia,
was still not ready,
but angry and
disappointed,
wanting to keep
traveling around the world,
saying she still had plenty
of places she wanted to visit.
When we asked her which ones,
she replied "Japan,"
for example.
After all, at 80, she
had been standing
at the Great Wall of China,

having found
a special low-priced tour
for seniors that the
Chinese government
was promoting at the time.
My brother gave her the money,
and off she went.
Although I'm grateful
for what I've been
able to experience so far —
publishing a book at 78,
seeing my son finally
receive his PhD
after years in grad school —
two of my strongest hopes,
I'd still like to have time
to publish another book or two
and see my son find a life partner,
although the next step,
being a grandparent,
is one I'll probably
not be around for,
my fault for having
waited so long to
be a parent.
Where would I like to be
and what would I like to be
doing when my time comes?
That answer is easy for me now.
When Allen Ginsberg
lay dying in his East Village
loft in Manhattan,

he was still writing,
surrounded by family
and many friends.
His last poem
was finished a few
days before he passed.
I don't need to have
a crowd around me,
just my immediates,
but like him,
I want to keep writing
to the end.

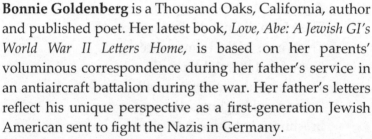

Bonnie Goldenberg is a Thousand Oaks, California, author and published poet. Her latest book, *Love, Abe: A Jewish GI's World War II Letters Home*, is based on her parents' voluminous correspondence during her father's service in an antiaircraft battalion during the war. Her father's letters reflect his unique perspective as a first-generation Jewish American sent to fight the Nazis in Germany.

She was formerly a labor attorney in New York and Washington, DC, and a writer and editor for a legal publisher in New York City. In addition to writing, she is the business administrator of her husband's biopharma startup in Newbury Park.

THE CRESCENT AND THE THISTLE

Claudine Mason-Marx

In my corner of the sky,
Beyond the trash cans, by and by,
Reclined a crescent, and to its rear,
A prickly thistle did appear.
The Moon did not disdain to face
This Venus of the human race.
I wonder if this sight installs
The peaceful slumber of us all . . .
Come regal brightness, beauty, wit,
Brashness, boldness, vanity, fit . . .
The Moon may peep upon the tides,
Unwary of the "could be" ides,
Reclining in the vast black sky,
Serene to our still open eye.

Claudine Mason-Marx is an enthusiastic substitute teacher, ballet instructor, wife, mother, and writer. She wrote her first poem in second grade, published in her school's newsletter, and has since written many poems, stories, and essays. Her poem "She" was featured in a Pasadena City College compilation of creative writing. In addition, her ballet dancing and choreography for the Gilbert and Sullivan musical *Iolanthe* elicited favorable reviews in local newspapers.

She is happy and grateful to be a member of Conejo Valley Writers, a group that has been a vital part of her growth as a writer. She hopes that her series of three children's books will be published in the not-so-distant future.

Claudine's hobbies include playing Catan with her husband and daughters, walking, reading, singing, snuggling with her cat, and playing online Jeopardy and Wordle.

ABYSS

Tamara Nowlin

In the eyes of possibility
I step into a sea of blue.
Reaching into the
ABYSS
Is where I encounter you.
You grab me tight
And pull me in
Springing hope that
Love will win.

JANUARY

Tamara Nowlin

I love how January is naked.
The trees stripped away
Revealing hidden bird's nest
Abandoned long ago.
Bare and exposed
Their true shape shines
And there is beauty
In the exposure
Beauty in the lack
Of pretense.
Beauty in their ability to grow
Despite their vulnerability.

SEEN

Tamara Nowlin

It is always the ocean
That speaks to me
In its beautiful softness
And simultaneous
violent ferocity.
I relate to that conflict
deep in my soul
the constant push and pull
of serene and unhinged
each time pulled back again.
Beautiful and calming

Tamara Nowlin was born and raised in Southern California. She obtained her BA in political science and sociology from Pepperdine University. After undergrad, she attended Southern Methodist University Law School in Dallas, Texas.

In her career she has enjoyed many roles, from attorney to school admissions to marketing and legal communications. She is also the founder of Yellow Daisy

Writers, a local writing services company specializing in content creation for small businesses, job seekers, and individuals.

Tamara has resided in Ventura County for the last twelve years with her two teenage children. She loves to travel, read, write poetry, and go to the beach, and is always up for an adventure.

WINTER

Alan Richard Zimmerman

Autumn turned to winter, little by little,
almost unnoticed from day to day.
What was the first sign? A bite of wind?
A snowflake's dance?
The first snowfall, smooth, untouched
A new horizon covering old ground
To watch, to listen — quiet, peaceful
A morning trance
But quickly trodden, shared by others
Day's light brought many changes
The snow toiled on, trying to recover
Its earlier glory
But one beginning seems the measure
of every season. Trying to gain
what was not lost, but what was first
A familiar story
White became the vision of a time, but white
was turning to gray as it always does
It was futile to try to stop the passing
Or so it seemed
Then night delivered a new beginning
Covering the footprints of the old work

Erasing memories of the old dawn
A paradise redeemed
It was a long winter but the cold air
and wet snow became kindred spirits
I treasured the print laden ground
All though December
But days made the scene seem common
One day as another, the wonder hidden in plain view.
It seemed there was nothing to forget
And yet nothing to remember.
Then the frozen sun called the thunder
And rain washed the snow from my sight
I tried in vain hoping the past
Could be extended
And at my feet, the last snowflake melted
I looked to the sky for a rainbow and
Saw only a gray cloud and I knew
That winter had ended.

Alan Richard Zimmerman was born, literally, on the banks of the Ohio River in West Virginia. Raised in West Virginia, he went to college in Arizona, and enjoyed a thirty-eight-year business career in Arizona and California. After retiring, Al moved back to Arizona to write and relax.

He has written and self-published novels, poetry, self-help works, short stories, comedy pieces, cartoons, and music.

To learn more, visit his website: www.ideajuicer.net.

LOOKING BACK IN TIME

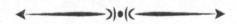

THE WORST DAY OF MY LIFE

Bob Calverley

————————◦◇◦————————

It was Wednesday, November 27, 1968—the day before Thanksgiving and the worst day of my life.

I was company clerk of the 187th Assault Helicopter Company, stationed in the Tây Ninh Base Camp, a few kilometers from Cambodia in the Republic of Vietnam. Overlooking the base camp, Núi Bà Đen (Black Virgin Mountain) is, at 3,268 feet, the highest mountain in Vietnam. It commands a verdant plain where a major branch of the Ho Chi Minh trail snakes into Vietnam from Cambodia on its way to Saigon.

That day our company was inserting the Fourth Battalion, Ninth Infantry "Manchus," part of the Twenty-fifth Infantry Division, into a landing zone (LZ) a scant two miles from Tây Ninh. Originating in 1855, the Fourth Battalion, Ninth Infantry regiment is one of the US Army's oldest units. The nickname Manchus stems from its deployment to China (1900-1901) to put down the Boxer Rebellion.

Outside the orderly room with a group of replacements who had just arrived, I marveled at the thundering American artillery barrage and watched air force fighter-bombers loft half a dozen 500-pound bombs onto the LZ. A helicopter streaked in at low level and laid down a thick curtain of oily smoke. Then our helicopter gunships raked the area with rockets and minigun fire.

After three months, I'd begun to feel like one of the luckiest draftees in Vietnam. No slogging through the jungle for me; I fought the enemy with an Underwood typewriter and a hand-cranked, temperamental mimeograph machine. We ate hot food, drank cold beer and sodas, slept on mattresses, and had sporadic electricity to power our stereos and box fans. Best of all, no one in the 187th had died in combat, though a few had suffered serious injuries, mostly in accidents. After seeing the preparation for the combat assault, I couldn't understand why overwhelming American firepower hadn't long ago defeated the Vietcong and North Vietnamese.

As a dozen of our helicopters, loaded with heavily armed grunts, sailed into the smoldering, smoky LZ, a North Vietnamese unit, consisting mostly of women, executed a meticulously planned ambush.

Small arms fire, rocket-propelled grenades (RPGs), and .51-caliber antiaircraft rounds erupted from all directions. An RPG struck the fuel cell of one helicopter, igniting a fireball that enveloped the machine and everyone in it. The Huey broke apart as it smashed into the ground, killing the twenty-year-old crew chief, Spec Four Jim Brady. Miraculously, the other three crew and all of the grunts on board would survive, though most were badly wounded.

After discharging his load of soldiers, and despite the withering fire, nineteen-year-old Warrant Officer Ron Timberlake circled back to pick up survivors. Timberlake's hootchmate, Chief Warrant Officer Bob Trezona, was aircraft commander of the downed ship. Overloaded with wounded survivors and heavily damaged by enemy fire, Timberlake's helicopter barely got off the ground before it, too, crashed a few hundred yards away. Other helicopters eventually rescued all of them.

The battle raged all day, as our helicopters flew in more infantry and took out the wounded and dead. We heard the explosions, the machine guns, the artillery, and the distinct slower, booming cadence of the .51. I shuddered at the body bags stacked beside the entrance of the MASH (mobile army surgical hospital) when I donated blood. I wondered if Brady lay among them.

Late in the afternoon, Sergeant Jerry Chandler called for volunteers to man a helicopter to drop flares. The desperate fight had continued into darkness. I volunteered. I wanted to do my part, and Brady was a friend. The night before, he and I had been drinking beer and talking about cars, family, and the rumored turkey dinner we'd heard we were getting for Thanksgiving. Many of us in the company occasionally flew as door gunners because we were chronically short of flight crews. Flying meant you earned an extra $65 a month. I'd already flown several missions, and we'd never been more in need than that day. Besides, when you're twenty-three years old, flying in a helicopter and manning a machine gun is a lot more fun than crafting reports that no one would ever read. And the flare ship would operate at 2,000 or 3,000 feet, out of range of most enemy weapons.

Well, there was that .51, but we'd heard it had been knocked out.

At the last minute, Chandler decided that he would fly instead of me. He was a sergeant and didn't feel right asking for volunteers without going himself.

The volunteer crew loaded the helicopter with thirty heavy parachute flares. On board were the aircraft commander, Warrant Officer Allen Duneman, twenty-five; copilot, Lieutenant August Ritzau, twenty-three, who had been wounded in the hand earlier in the day; and door gunners Spec Four Fred Frazer, twenty-one, who had just returned from a thirty-day leave after extending his tour of duty six months; Spec Four Dave Creel, an avionics technician; and Chandler, who was twenty-four. He would eject the flares.

The flare ship had just reached 3,000 feet when Duneman suddenly screamed for help over the radio. A flare on the bottom of the stack had ignited. The flares burned a magnesium compound, emitting two million candlepower of light. Once lit, they are impossible to extinguish and so bright the two pilots could not see outside, nor could they see their instruments. Magnesium burns at 4,000 degrees and the flares were stacked on top of a fuel cell. Helicopter frames are made from a magnesium alloy that, when hot enough, will burn.

Later, an investigation would conclude that enemy ground fire ignited the flare, but it could have been an accident. None of the pilots or crew had any experience with flares. Experienced crews were all fighting in the battle. A work order with instructions on a new way to affix flares to the outside of a helicopter sat unread in the maintenance inbox. The modification would have allowed pilots to jettison the flares.

Duneman dove for the ground while a pilot in another helicopter radioed altitude readings to him. More flares began to ignite.

"Four hundred feet! Pull up! Pull up!" But the helicopter slammed into the ground, exploding in a white-hot conflagration of JP-4 fuel and magnesium. All five men on board died.

That day we suffered six dead and more than twenty badly wounded. We had only three flyable helicopters at the end of the day, and the 187th was effectively out of action. Twenty-seven of the Manchus died in the fight and sixty were wounded. At that time, regulations prohibited unarmed medevacs from landing in a hot LZ, so all the wounded were flown out by our helicopters.

The Thanksgiving dinner never materialized. The enemy also ambushed the truck convoy carrying turkeys to Tây Ninh. We ate something tasting vaguely like chicken.

The two pilots of the ship hit by the RPG both suffered third-degree burns over fifty percent of their bodies and neither was expected to live. However, both not only survived but they thrived. After sixty-three surgeries, Trezona married and had children and grandchildren. He became one of the West's most sought-after saddlemakers. Lieutenant Tom Pienta, who had slightly fewer surgeries, wrote a first-person account, *Trial by Fire*, about his experience. It was published as the cover story in the December 1996 issue of *Vietnam* magazine. Pienta has attended several of our reunions, and we exchange emails sometimes.

Fifteen years ago, Trezona got as far as the hallway outside of the hospitality suite at one of our reunions. But he couldn't bring himself to enter and see his friends. His wounds had left him with a hideously scarred face. He passed away in 2019.

A few years ago, I spoke to Jerry Chandler's son by telephone for more than an hour, and barely remember the conversation. He was desperate to speak to anyone who had known his father, who had died before he was born. He'd made the army his career and was a special forces ranger in Colombia. I know his father would have been proud.

I often think about Chandler and how close I came to dying. I think about all of them and of the life I've had and the one they missed.

That was the day before Thanksgiving, the worst day of my life, a life that I am so very grateful to have had.

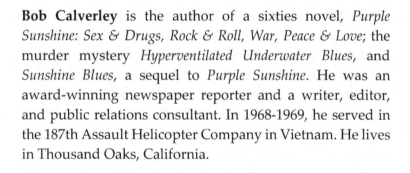

Bob Calverley is the author of a sixties novel, *Purple Sunshine: Sex & Drugs, Rock & Roll, War, Peace & Love*; the murder mystery *Hyperventilated Underwater Blues*, and *Sunshine Blues*, a sequel to *Purple Sunshine*. He was an award-winning newspaper reporter and a writer, editor, and public relations consultant. In 1968-1969, he served in the 187th Assault Helicopter Company in Vietnam. He lives in Thousand Oaks, California.

ONCE A KID FROM BROOKLYN

Michael Edelstein

———————◦◇◦———————

I was once a kid from Brooklyn—East New York and Brownsville neighborhoods, to be specific. I was born in Bushwick Hospital on February 5, 1939, a tumultuous year. It was the same day that Generalissimo Francisco Franco anointed himself *caudillo* (military dictator) of Spain, and less than a month before Hitler's Germany invaded Czechoslovakia.

I lived with my mom and dad for about a year on Howard Avenue, north of Livonia Avenue, with its elevated IRT tracks. There, at eight weeks of age, I was roughly introduced to the rigors of religion at my bris (ritual circumcision), immediately calling to my attention the failings of observance.

At fifteen months of my new life, we moved to 236-8 New Jersey Avenue, between Liberty and Glenmore Avenues. There we pronounced it "Nu Joisey Av." I much later learned middle-American newspeak, and all the earl and shuggah were transmuted to oil and sugar, the latter served with coffee, not cawfeee, and Williamsboig and New Joisey dropped their oi's in favor of ur's and er's.

At the time, East New York was known as the Little Italy of Brooklyn, with most of our ENY neighbors being first-generation or recent immigrants of Italian descent; and Brownsville was known as the manager of Murder Inc., as well as the home mostly of Jews from Eastern Europe, a.k.a. Ashkenazim.

Early on, I knew nothing of Christians and/or Jews and even less of denominations. It was Us and Them. I thought that all Christians were Italian and all Italians were Christian-Catholics. That included the Russian émigrés who attended the Russian Orthodox Church around the corner, the bells of which awakened me early Sunday mornings, and the (Polish) Sadowskis and Pupkowskis on the ground and fourth floors of our four-floor walk-up tenement.

There were two or three trees, spindly "mapleoids" with a smidgen of dirt around them, on our side of the block, and two large sycamores directly across the street from our tenement home, in front of the Lutheran church, whose bells were softer than those of the Russian church. On their tiny plots of dirt, we played marbles, out of the gutter, and mumblety-peg.

There was also a minimal plot of grass in front of the Lutheran church, surrounded by the picket fence on which my right thigh became painfully impaled at age seven and I closely avoided emasculation. I had attempted to climb over the fence to retrieve a pink Spaldeen (Spalding) ball, lost by an errantly thrown punchball. It was then that I was introduced to emergency room medicine, at the Lutheran hospital on Atlantic Avenue, where the gaping wound in my right thigh was sutured closed, with the admonition "Don't ever do that again."

An occasional weed shot up between the cracks of the slate sidewalk in front of our house, where it joined the concrete that had been recently poured. To round out the verdant element within our neighborhood, window boxes sported red geraniums during the warmer months and dead sticks in the winter.

~ ~ ~

Worn stairs led up to our second-floor apartment, number four, next to the dumbwaiter, with its myriad intrusions of cockroaches. The halls were lit only by ambient light floating in through dusty, grimy mid-wall windows, and a faint, often flickering 30-watt bulb at night. The landings were covered in white, hexagonal one-and-a-half-inch tiles, and the stairs were made of tired gray granite, which wanted scrubbing.

The halls were redolent with the scents of recipes from Ukraine, Poland, Russia, and Italy, having a strong dependency on garlic and onions, with an overlay of tomato on one side and cabbage on the other. Doors were left open for apartment ventilation, emitting an aroma that blissfully scented out, "Home."

I "second-started" school at PS 63 on Williams Avenue at age five, walking five blocks east on Glenmore Avenue. each morning, and back, walking west on Liberty Avenue, the latter after General Motors bought the trolley line and did away with the electric power overhead so that buses could blow their exhaust fumes our way to ready us for adulthood. We strode past the Piels Beer brewery, with its runoff puddles of beer spilling out onto the sidewalk and into the air with their heady scent, thankfully obscuring the exhaust fumes.

I'll take a step back to my premier start at school. I didn't want to reveal this, but I really began kindergarten at PS 173, around the corner, at age four and a half; too young to avoid juvenile apprenticeship to a second-grade arsonist, who set newspapers on fire in a cellar staircase, bringing me unearned notoriety and record time expulsion from that pre-madrassa. I hold the record for the shortest stay in kindergarten (one week) before expulsion.

The streets wore cobbles until sometime after World War II, when black asphalt was poured over the stones and the residue of the many horse-drawn carts that delivered fruit, vegetables, ice, and seltzer to our doors. It did not smell so great, but it improved the playing field between the sewers for stickball, punchball, ring-a-levio, and kick the can.

My forty-square-foot room, a little larger than today's workplace cubicle, sat at the rear of our seven hundred-square-foot apartment, with its own useless steam pipe for winter heat and a fire escape at the rear, which we used for summer sleeping in Brooklyn's scald and as a repository for the case of seltzer on which we thrived.

My direct view was the back side of a schoolyard, PS 173, which became a girls' high school, allowing adolescent me to happily watch teenage girls bounce and stretch in their green gym uniforms as they played volleyball in the summer, surrounded by a lanai safety screen of wire atop the school's gymnasium.

It was in an alcove of that same school building that we boys played handball against its wall—at every possible summer moment away from work—pounding our pink balls, scrambling, and diving, with all our might.

The edifice was fronted by a sixty-by-sixty elevated foot athletic field over a cemented base, which roughly took swatches of epidermis from my legs. It was here that we tossed a football in the fall, when breaks in inclement weather allowed, and I watched tall teen boys play basketball at the north end of the field against backless, un-netted metal hoops. I would have played as well, but was prohibited by asthma, not easily treated until the 1970s brought us handy inhalers of beta-agonists (by which time I was a Californian and began jogging, which led to running and advanced to marathons).

In the northwest corner of the concrete-skinned lot on which our tenement stood, also visible from my bedroom window, rose a two-story wooden pole, which carried electrical and telephone lines into the house and bore clotheslines that we filled every few days with our colorful clothing pennants and pale bed linens through our living room window, after scrubbing them on the corrugated washboard in our kitchen washtub (in which we also bathed my infant sister, Judy). My recall of it tickled me when, in the navy, my memory compared our drying wash to flying semaphore flags.

Through that same window, I could peer due north to Liberty Avenue across rows of semidetached gray brick duplexes with their tiny unplanted backyards, emblematic of our working-class/lower middle-class precinct, to Nilo's barbershop on one corner and the Williamsburg Savings Bank on the other.

Dr. Michael Edelstein, MD, MBA, practiced medicine from 1962 through 2015. He has written and read poetry for as long as he can remember. He was Brooklyn JHS 149's 1950 Poet Laureate and still has the medal to show for it.

Dr. Edelstein has retired to a career in writing, especially as a poet; and is working on a prose-poetry memoir, "A Doctor's Journey through Strokeland."

WAKING UP

Mark Frankcom

————————◦❦◦————————

I woke up to the buzzing and frightening noise of a CT machine scanning my brain. Music was playing, I guess to calm me down. But it was so claustrophobic and horribly oppressive, all I wanted to do was get out of there.

Why was I here? What had happened?

My mother had found me. She described it as the worst day of her life. Me, unconscious, on the floor in the bedroom upstairs in her house. She called 999, which in England is the equivalent of 911 in America. The ambulance responded very quickly. A helicopter flew a doctor out; they examined me and decided I needed to go the hospital.

Later, I learned I'd had a stroke at the age of sixty and had been in a coma for two weeks. Two weeks! Not a conventional stroke, either. Rather, it was a brain bleed from a cavernoma, a cavernous malformation inside the middle of my brain. And it was so dangerous they couldn't operate, because it was close to everything your brain controls. They had put a shunt in my head, which is supposed to drain fluid and take away pressure so you can function again.

I was lying in a hospital bed in Southampton, England, pretty out of it. My wife had flown in ten hours, from Los Angeles to London. A long time to be worrying about me lying there. She and my mother had been visiting the hospital every day for two weeks. My son, who lives in London, also came to the hospital. I recalled nothing about this. I guess I just dreamed; I'm not sure now about what. I must have had pretty strong reactions to a strange new place, but the brain, your memory, does a pretty good job of making you forget all that.

I was lying in a hospital bed surrounded by a lot of other people with strange contraptions on their heads. When I went to sleep at night, or tried to sleep, I could hear screaming. The screaming of a lady, obviously in distress, who wanted to get out of there. The nurses were running around trying to keep her quiet, to let the rest of us sleep. Sleep was not easily coming.

After lying there for two weeks, it was decided the shunt was not working. I was getting worse, not better. A doctor there (one of these days I will find out who you are and thank you personally), determined that I needed an operation. He inserted a mechanical shunt, which drains the blood from your brain into your thorax, and then the very poisonous liquid dissolves, or so I was told (in some way which I don't understand). And it worked. A mechanical shunt doesn't need a battery and doesn't set off alarms at the airport, which is probably just as well. I will have it for the rest of my life.

When my wife—who had been told by the doctor that I would be paralyzed and unable to speak, etc.—felt me hug her, she was very emotional. I can't remember very much of that time. She and my mother were given lots of very bad predictions. Both had to contend with the fact that maybe I wasn't going to be very much use to anybody in the future. The new reality: I was disabled. I had no sense of balance.

My body felt very heavy when I tried to move. I was very wobbly on my journey to the bathroom, and nearly fell over a number of times. That feeling has stayed with me ever since. I was lucky. I wasn't paralyzed and I could speak, but I could only walk with great effort.

I spent another four weeks in the hospital. One day when my wife came to visit, she held me and, with my right arm, I was able to hold and hug her.

I was relocated to the Queen Alexandra Hospital in Portsmouth, in southern England, and was there for four more weeks in a private rehab ward, initially, which was very nice. Then I was moved to a public ward, somewhat less nice: a hospital bed in an area with lots of other people in various medical conditions, from bad to very bad.

Through all that, my strongest memory is waking up in that machine. And that wake up was also a wake-up call for my life ahead. Waking up—not just actually opening my eyes, but also waking up to a new disabled reality.

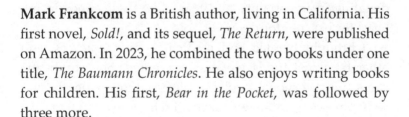

Mark Frankcom is a British author, living in California. His first novel, *Sold!*, and its sequel, *The Return*, were published on Amazon. In 2023, he combined the two books under one title, *The Baumann Chronicles*. He also enjoys writing books for children. His first, *Bear in the Pocket*, was followed by three more.

Mark's wife, Margret, also an author of children's books, is German, and they have three children. The Frankcoms are both very involved with nonprofit organizations that support disabled or mentally challenged children.

LILAC SKY

Claudine Mason-Marx

———————◦◇◦———————

The day started out gray, rainy, and onerous, with yet another of the many illnesses confining her to bed in the morning. Fever swept over her once again. No COVID, at least, which she'd had last year; no stomach flu, again like earlier this year. But chills and fever held her in hostility, only relenting as the day progressed. The next morning, the two symptoms grabbed her in their clutches once more—easing as the day went on—and so the pattern repeated for eight days, with yet more school missed. I heard none of her beautiful music on saxophone or piano during this time. Sometimes the house was bathed in a silence that hung dangling in uncertainty and fear—like the feelings in my heart for her, my fourteen-year-old.

I brought her tea and medicine—fruit, crackers, and other breakfast foods when she accepted. She taught me chess one afternoon, explaining everything patiently and well. The second time we played, I felt more confident. The third, she agreed I did much better and sent me a video so that I might improve my game further. We hadn't played anything in quite a while, and even though I wanted her in school, it was the silver lining of sickness.

In the sky, toward the end of her illness, a streak of white cumulus clouds appeared, fluffy and loose, freed of the white sandwich of dense, static gases. Dark lilac clouds burst forth in the gray sky, exquisite in their sublime hue, the memory of which overshadows the long, oppressive, lilac clump that appeared days later.

My wish for her and my other daughter would be to burst through the grayness of illness and any other obstacle. May they shine healthy, happy, enthusiastic, and optimistic as the lilac sky.

Claudine Mason-Marx is an enthusiastic substitute teacher, ballet instructor, wife, mother, and writer. She wrote her first poem in second grade, published in her school's newsletter, and has since written many poems, stories, and essays. Her poem "She" was featured in a Pasadena City College compilation of creative writing. In addition, her ballet dancing and choreography for the Gilbert and Sullivan musical *Iolanthe* elicited favorable reviews in local newspapers.

She is happy and grateful to be a member of Conejo Valley Writers, a group that has been a vital part of her growth as a writer. She hopes that her series of three children's books will be published in the not-so-distant future.

Claudine's hobbies include playing Catan with her husband and daughters, walking, reading, singing, snuggling with her cat, and playing online Jeopardy and Wordle.

MY TEN-YEAR JOURNEY TO "AUTHORDOM"

Stephen Marks

The journey started in 2011, but the trigger came in 2005. In 2011, it was seven years since I learned my then three-year-old niece in Reno, NV had contracted type 1 diabetes. And over the next many years, I witnessed how devastating this life-threatening and life-altering diagnosis proved to be, both for her and for the people that cared for and about her.

In 2008 she moved back from Reno to Thousand Oaks, California, and we started spending time together. The more time we spent together, I came to understand her situation. I felt compelled to do "something."

Shortly thereafter, I saw an article in our local newspaper, the Thousand Oaks *News-Chronicle,* about a local Ventura County sheriff's deputy, Randy Pentis, whose son was a type 1 diabetic. Randy had started a fundraising group called Cops Riding for Charity. He and a few others—eight if I remember correctly—would travel the world every year with their bicycles and ride hundreds of miles in the outermost areas of civilization. Their mission was to raise money for an organization formerly known as the Juvenile Diabetes Research Foundation, and currently known as JDRF.

Why the name change? Because kids having contracted type 1 were living longer as a result of better treatment protocols. The numbers of type 1 adolescents and adults that needed support was growing.

I wrote Cops Riding for Charity a check for $500 after calling Randy and learning more about his efforts and his passion. I donated to his cause for four years, when the rides stopped. Time had caught up with his riders.

Randy introduced me to a woman named Elizabeth, their JDRF liaison. She educated me on the disease and how JDRF supported the T1D community through advocacy and fundraising. She invited me to a few events they sponsored. I was humbled learning how big the type 1 community was, the magnitude of the devastation of the disease, and that tens of thousands of people in some fashion connected to type 1 diabetics gave their time and gave their money.

I decided that Starnet (the company I owned for thirty-one years) would become involved with JDRF and T1D advocacy. I started our Rebate for Charity program and donated a percentage of qualifying sales. We funded these donations for five years, and they totaled over $200,000.

Because of the big numbers we donated, JDRF invited me to join their Los Angeles board of directors. I participated from 2011 to 2017. While on the board, I learned more about the disease, new treatments, and technological developments. I also learned the medical research community did not know what caused the condition, and a cure was still far off in the distance. Unfortunately, in 2023, this is still the case.

I was frustrated, and wanted to do more, and became involved in JDRF board committees. I involved myself in many fundraising and awareness activities, and it was gratifying. But it was also frustrating that all of JDRF's "macro" efforts seemed somewhat remote from the actual day-to-day existence of my niece and all the others that were suffering with the disease.

I wanted to do more, and in 2011 the idea of a story came to me. I felt inspired to write how, despite millions of dollars in medical research funding, there was, and still is, uncertainty as to the cause. And no cure. I felt inspired to write about different outcomes. I wasn't educated in the art of storytelling, but I started anyway. My thought was, "Steve you're a smart guy–you'll figure it out. But you've got to get going." So, I got going. It was a slow start, as I wrote a little at a time. The story was in my head, but I was uncertain how to lay the words down. And I was busy running a business, giving me numerous excuses not to write. But not the real reason.

By 2013, I had a hundred pages written, then stopped. Looking back, there were three reasons I put the manuscript "in the drawer." My niece, now twelve, had moved to Las Vegas. Suddenly, her relationship with her uncle was not as important to her as when she was younger. My contacts with her slowed, and then stopped as she moved into adolescence. We had lost touch.

Second, she had now been living with type 1 diabetes for ten years. The reality of her life had settled in for her and for all of us that cared for and about her. There was not as much passion in fighting. Her battles with T1D life— pricking fingers, testing blood, taking shots of insulin, counting carbohydrates—had become normalized. It was also a life of often not feeling well. For us who cared for and loved her, our thoughts were of her survival and an uncertain future. The uncertainty was unsettling. What would be the long-term effects of self-regulating her blood glucose levels instead of having a healthy and functioning pancreas doing so? But these fears had been with us for many years, and over time they waned.

With recent reflection, the third and perhaps the most impactful reason I stopped writing in 2014 was because, subconsciously, I knew I wasn't prepared to tell the story effectively. I had convinced myself discreetly that my story wasn't worth telling if it could not be told well. The manuscript sat dormant for seven years, from 2013 to 2020. Whether I would ever finish it had become a fleeting thought. That is until retirement happened, thanks in large part to COVID-19.

In April of 2020, I found myself with lots of time and relieved from the stresses of owning and operating a business. And with a renewed interest in telling the story I always thought was one worth telling. So, I started writing again. And I started studying the art of storytelling. With the knowledge of what it takes to tell a good story with written words, and tell it well, I found the renewed sense of purpose and passion I had lost seven years earlier.

In 2020, thanks to newfound availability of time and newly acquired knowledge, I upped my game and started writing at a feverish pace. The story rushed through me and onto the laptop screen. And it was, to my thinking, good.

In September 2020, I wrote "The End" to a completed first draft consisting of 127,000 words and 440 pages. In April 2022, after no less than twenty rewrites, professional developmental editing, professional copyediting, professional cover design and professional formatting, we hit the Publish button.

And now, it's on to a new journey: convincing readers this story is worthy of their time. For that purpose, I built a website and started a blog, both from the point of view of our hero, the fictional (unfortunately) Jonathon Braxton. And our hero is also using social media through accounts created in his name and voice.

In telling Jon's story, I included numerous conversations and controversial positions on a few of the social issues we face today. Jon Braxton, on his way to finding the cure to T1D, unintentionally manages to turn Washington, DC, upside down while bringing both the Republican and Democratid parties to the brink of extinction.

For those of you in the type 1 community, my hope is you will find hope and inspiration in my words, that there is a cure for T1D on the horizon. And all it takes to bring it in is a guy like JB to shake things up.

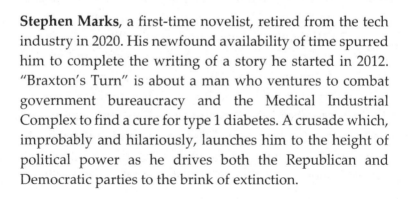

Stephen Marks, a first-time novelist, retired from the tech industry in 2020. His newfound availability of time spurred him to complete the writing of a story he started in 2012. "Braxton's Turn" is about a man who ventures to combat government bureaucracy and the Medical Industrial Complex to find a cure for type 1 diabetes. A crusade which, improbably and hilariously, launches him to the height of political power as he drives both the Republican and Democratic parties to the brink of extinction.

He lives in Thousand Oaks, California, and is currently writing the sequel to *Braxton's Time* and is working with a Hollywood producer to have his story adapted as a streaming network series.

AUGIE

Judy Panczak

————————◇◆◇◦————————

I met Augie when he married my Aunt Bobbie. Now in her forties, this was her first marriage, so I was curious to meet her new husband and congratulate them both. Our time with them was limited but pleasant. They seemed quite happy.

While on summer vacation the following year, Bobbie and Augie invited our family to see the ranch they purchased. We noticed they were drinking quite heavily, which I found very disturbing, since they wanted us to extend our visit for several days. We spent the night but made an excuse to leave the next morning. Their arguing and drinking created an environment I did not need my children to experience.

When Augie married Bobbie, she was a very emotionally destructive alcoholic, and he was equally emotionally destructive to her. He is dead now, so I feel free to tell you his story in hopes that it may help another. I loved his humor and the sadness of him.

As a youth, Augie hunted and farmed in Minnesota, where he was born. He was "Minnesota nice": courteous, reserved, mild-mannered, and passive-aggressive against people who were not like him. If Augie was drinking and made backhanded comments to Bobbie, he could sulk, withdraw, and not communicate.

He graduated from college and attempted a career in journalism, but not successfully, so he sought success as a salesman for a stationary company.

Augie met and married Bobbie, a very successful sportswear buyer with a job at a prominent clothing company, late in life after his first wife's death.

She was his drinking buddy. They had fun together, and the "fun" always included drinking, jokes, laughing, and trips to Lake Tahoe. Bobbie bragged that she married a pencil salesman, but in fact, Augie was quite successful in sales and real estate investments. He showed her love by being affectionate and caring for their properties. Their marriage "joking" was trading off sarcastic barbs, and as the drinking progressed, Bobbie proceeded to one-up Augie's sarcasm to the point of destroying his masculinity with comments like "I make more money than you do."

In retaliation for the criticisms and arguments, he quit working and decided to live off his inheritance and continued his new career: drinking.

Their marriage continued to have its ups and downs. His favorite pastime was purchasing different ethnic hats, which he would model and portray the role it represented. He would be a bullfighter one day and on safari the next— this was his escape. They bought a ranchito near Sebastopol, California, and named it Rancho Costa Plenti. Maybe he couldn't or wouldn't work, but he sure knew how to successfully invest. I think she knew it too. Bobbie felt guilty about all the arguments and tried to make it up to him. She decided to buy him five cows, one of which she named Bobita to humor Augie.

Soon he was wearing cowboy outfits, and his drinking became worse. He sought treatment at a facility which he named the "funny farm," to regain sobriety, but that was unsuccessful. Augie made several more attempts at numerous facilities. While at the facilities, every morning he loved raising the flag, while calling himself a great "scoutmaster."

As time progressed, his alcoholism worsened and his behavior became more erratic. He would sleepwalk and roam around the ranchito all night or sit in the barn and talk to the cows. He alienated all his friends with cruel criticisms and impatience.

The last I heard about Augie, he decided to take a trip to Tahoe to see a nephew. After not hearing from him, Bobbie went to seek him out and found him dead in the Tahoe cabin. The autopsy result was death from a hepatic coma, a sad ending to an erratic life. So much potential lost to alcoholism.

Bobbie also developed cirrhosis of the liver, and she died soon after. Out of her five siblings, two brothers had PTSD from World War II, and a sister also died. Bobbie also had two uncles who were in World War I who also had PTSD, and they died of alcoholism and homelessness. One sister died of cancer. In the next generation, one son committed suicide and was an alcoholic. His father was an alcoholic. Two other grandchildren socially drink. So many alcoholics are treatment resistant, saying, "I can take care of this on my own." How did this this gentleman create and progress to this? And so, I reminisce with a poem:

To Augie

Five cows awaiting in the pasture for a friend not far away, and now they are gone and so is he, how sad it is today.

Our Midnight Cowboy have you found the meaning now?

Have you found a friend, a partner with your love Bobita cow?

Share your peace with us. We suffer here on Earth.

We will remember all the good times and remember your worth.

Have a good walk, and the road will take you there.

You've played the game well; you've taken the dare.

There are things that I know to be true about alcoholism, coming from a family of them. I know it's nature and nurture that affects us. Nature, meaning what we genetically inherit. Nurture, meaning how we thrived pre- and post-birth, how we were parented, and the trauma we endured in life.

Here are some statistics:

- 90% of those with alcohol addiction started drinking before age 18.
- Six people die every minute because of harmful alcohol.
- A blood alcohol level of .08 can get you arrested and put in jail, with a total legal expense of up to $30,000.
- A blood alcohol level of .30 can cause a coma.
- A blood alcohol level of .40 can cause death.
- Even though alcohol may induce some good feelings, it is a depressant.
- Alcohol affects men and women differently: carbonated drinks increase the rate of alcohol absorption.

- The pressure inside the stomach and small intestine forces the alcohol to be absorbed more quickly into the bloodstream.

The Mayo Clinic asks:

✓ When you decided to stop drinking for a week or so, did sobriety only last for a couple of days?

✓ Have you had to drink upon waking up during the past year?

✓ Does your drinking cause trouble at home?

✓ Have you missed days of work or school because of drinking?

✓ Have you ever felt that your life would be better if you did not drink?

If you answered yes, you might have a dysfunctional relationship with alcohol; consider getting help. Professionals suggest being in the right mind to get sober. The first step of Alcoholics Anonymous is: "I honestly admit that I am powerless over alcohol and that my life has become unmanageable." This is when you are ready for sobriety. There is no quick fix. It may take several attempts.

A doctor may prescribe antidepressants or anxiety medication, but you have to carefully watch for side effects. Mixing alcohol with medication increases their potency four times. Treatment should always include therapy, and it is not as effective without it. In other words, you have to be courageous to follow the path to sobriety.

The Mayo Clinic also says symptoms of alcohol abuse can include hangovers, slow reaction times, poor and double vision, upset stomach, depression, memory loss, and coma. Alcohol abuse can affect your personal relationships, finances, your job, and your health. Unfortunately, when you drink, it doesn't only interfere with your life, it cuts into the quality of life for those around you. Drinking too much can cause poor judgment and impaired decision-making ability. This can cause those who spend time around you to have to pay for your mistakes and bad decisions. Eventually, people may want to stop spending time with you.

If you or someone you know is struggling with alcohol abuse don't wait.

CALL NOW

Suicide Prevention Hotline

Phone: 988

Internet 988 lifeline.org

Local Alcoholics Anonymous

Phone number 805-522-1300

Internet: AA.org

National Drug and Alcohol treatment hotline 1-800 662-4357

Drugabuse.com

If what I have written can salvage one life, I feel like I have accomplished my quest to heal the generational effect of alcoholism

I remember seeing a thirty-one-year-old cancer patient named NIGHTBIRD who gave a wonderful inspirational message about her cancer, that I think can also be related to alcoholism. "You can't wait until life isn't hard anymore before you decide to be happy."

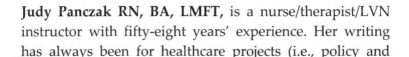

Judy Panczak RN, BA, LMFT, is a nurse/therapist/LVN instructor with fifty-eight years' experience. Her writing has always been for healthcare projects (i.e., policy and

procedure manuals, performance reviews, and reports). She became interested in the Conejo Valley Writers when she was trying to write a family cookbook. However, the group has since challenged her to write more, and has become a pleasant re-engaging social experience since her husband's passing.

She has lived in Westlake Village, California, for over forty-four years, is the mother of three sons, and grandmother of eleven.

PAPER DOLLS

Kathleen Galloway Rogan

It was around the time of Yardley cosmetics, the models Jean Shrimpton and Twiggy, but the biggest influence was the British Invasion of rock music.

The setting was a fashion and music happening: Mod Festival '67 at the Hollywood Palladium, on March 17, Saint Patrick's Day.

"Wonderful Mother," as she called herself, dropped me and one of my best pals, Stephanie, off at the Mod Festival. She drove off in her maroon Oldsmobile Toronado, cigarette in her hand and vodka hidden to no one in her coffee mug. "Auntie Mame" was more like it, as she gave us a brisk and haughty, "Have fun, girls, but not too much fun!" I watched her speed away, never looking back.

The Beatles, Stones, Kinks, Yardbirds, The Who, Herman's Hermits, and Gerry and the Pacemakers were playing on the loudspeakers. Fashion shows, makeup vendors, pop-up dress shops, and all the fish 'n' chips one could eat. I was wearing my lime-green, sleeveless paper dress and white patent leather go-go boots. My bangs covering my eyebrows and very long, surfer-straight hair were the envy of all my curly-haired friends. I had cat eyes, green eye shadow, fake eyelashes, and white lipstick. I did also own a black-and-white mock-newspaper paper dress, but since it was Saint Paddy's Day, the green dress was the obvious choice!

Stephanie was wearing a tight, bright pink poor boy T-shirt, pink floral miniskirt, and a wide Barbie-pink plastic belt, with matching T-strap patent leather sandals. Her hair in the universal style like mine: straight, parted down the middle, with a long, heavy bang. Her makeup was the same London look as mine, except for a pale pink lip.

We were in absolute heaven trying on clothes and shoes, getting makeovers, enjoying the fashion/music bonanza taking place, when suddenly we were thirsty.

There was a pub set up at the back of the Palladium, next to the stage, and we slipped in on the side. Gerry and the Pacemakers had just performed "Ferry Cross the Mersey," and Gerry Marsden and his brother Freddie walked into the pub for a pint after their set.

Stephanie and I couldn't stop staring at the guys, so Gerry just came over to our table and said, "You can say hello, you know. We ain't goin' to bite cha!" We just blushed for too long, then got out a tiny "hi" and "hello." Freddie came over to join us and said, "Would either of you lasses like to visit us on our break?"

Like to? Oh my God! Heaven opened up! Gerry went up the bar and ordered four pints of beer. We were both fourteen, looking twenty-one, so no one carded us. We were giddy; it was all set to be a bossa nova groovy time indeed!

We all cracked up as I told Gerry my favorite song was "Don't Let the Sun Catch You Crying" and I had the Pacemakers' band poster on the inside of my closet door. I also divulged kissing his photo good night before I went to sleep.

Freddie and Stephanie were really hitting it off too. We wound up meeting up with them again after their last set and making out in the posh conversation pits set up around the stage.

As far as Saint Patrick's Day celebrations go, this was by far the most fabulous one indeed. I had my first beer, first kiss, and all in a green paper dress!

Our ride returned, Mom in her moving ashtray, to drive us back to the suburbs north of Los Angeles. We giggled and sang the Pacemakers' other big hit, "You You You," until my mom started complaining, "Oh for Christ's sake, girls! Seven times is enough! You are both so silly!" and put Frank Sinatra on the radio, while blowing smoke out the window. We didn't care, for I knew I'd be seeing my new boyfriend—Gerry, the Pacemakers' lead singer from Liverpool—soon on my closet door.

Oh yeah, promises were made for when they'd be back in town, etc., but who knows if anything will happen with the boys again? If it doesn't, we'll always have Mod Festival '67.

Kathleen Galloway Rogan, a writer, performer, and teacher, was born Kathleen Teresa Galloway in New York City on May 28, 1953. She grew up in Southern California and attended California Institute of the Arts from 1993 to 1998, earning both a bachelor of fine arts and a master of fine arts degree.

A writer of plays, short stories, stand-up, and memoir, Kathleen has performed in commedia dell'arte in Santa Barbara, *The Vagina Monologues* at Moorpark College, and various evenings of one-acts at Moorpark College and The Mayflower Club Celtic Arts Center in North Hollywood.

She has taught creative writing at the Conejo Valley Adult School for the last seventeen years. A substitute teacher for the Los Angeles School District eight years standing, Kathleen has been married for thirty-seven years and has two grown sons.

DIARY OF A WIMPY CAMPER

Marcia Smart

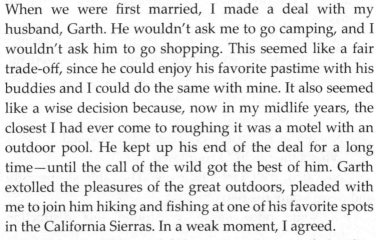

When we were first married, I made a deal with my husband, Garth. He wouldn't ask me to go camping, and I wouldn't ask him to go shopping. This seemed like a fair trade-off, since he could enjoy his favorite pastime with his buddies and I could do the same with mine. It also seemed like a wise decision because, now in my midlife years, the closest I had ever come to roughing it was a motel with an outdoor pool. He kept up his end of the deal for a long time—until the call of the wild got the best of him. Garth extolled the pleasures of the great outdoors, pleaded with me to join him hiking and fishing at one of his favorite spots in the California Sierras. In a weak moment, I agreed.

I didn't really mind hiking. It was one of the few outdoor activities I enjoyed—unless it took place in woods that teemed with wildlife whose bite required emergency evacuation. But I wasn't sold on fishing. My only recollection of that activity was when I threw a ping-pong ball in a bowl and won a goldfish at a carnival. I also worried about sleeping arrangements. I'd already paid for my chiropractor's new car, so huddled in a bag on the ground was a deal breaker. The more I thought about it, the less attractive the camping excursion became.

Determined to discourage Garth from pressing the issue, I created a fool-proof prerequisite list and presented it to him.

"I'll do it, as long as there is a sink with running water, a stove to cook on, a bed to sleep in and an indoor bathroom . . . with a shower."

"Can it be a group shower/bathroom facility?" he asked.

"No way—private or nothing." I was sure I had him on that one.

A few days went by and I heard nothing more about the camping adventure. I relaxed, convinced I'd delivered an impossible request.

My Meriwether Lewis was not daunted. "OK, I found a place that meets all your requirements." He handed me information on the campsite, complete with photo of an A-frame cabin nestled among some trees.

"I see woods." I said.

"Not dense, just scattered trees." He answered.

"What's the catch?" I countered.

"No catch. Well, just a little one. The cabin sleeps eight and there's only the two of us."

For some odd reason, he found this distinction ridiculous.

"Perfect." I groaned and sealed the deal.

~~~

We arrived at the A-frame that would be our "camp" for the next week. My hubby opened the door and said, "Wow. This is awesome. What a great place."

I stood in the doorway, stunned into silence.

The old wooden floors had so many layers of earth ground into them they were now part of the décor. A wall, black with soot, surrounded a pot-bellied stove which required wood to be chopped and hauled inside to heat the cabin. Greasy kitchen cabinets sported threadbare fabric door fronts, which hid dented pans and hard plastic dishes. Dirt being my nemesis, I was afraid to touch anything. When I spotted a questionable vermin carcass on the floor in the corner—horror struck. Ready to bolt out the door, I remembered my promise to Garth.

Resigned to my fate, I resolved to be a good sport, put on my happy camper face, gave a soft "uhmmmm" in agreement with his enthusiasm, asked him to please remove the dead critter. At least I had my indoor toilette.

The next morning, I swaddled my feet in moleskin. This was an important precaution to prevent blisters from the hiking boots that I had only worn twice before. It didn't help.

We headed for the hills, hiking to hubby's favorite fishing spot. I looked away as he positioned the poor little worm on my hook. I followed his instructions and cast my line out as far as I was able. Beginner's luck, I hooked the first fish—a nice trout.

The resistance of the fish as it struggled on the line made me shudder. I eased off and gently tugged on the pole.

"Harder," Garth yelled. "Pull it in, pull it in . . . harder."

I envisioned the harpoonlike hook mercilessly caught in trout lips. "But I don't want to hurt the fish," I whined in response.

"Don't be ridiculous. Just reel him in. Fish don't have any feeling in their mouths," declared Mr. Heartless Fish Expert.

"How do you know? You're not a fish." I flashed on *The Old Man and the Sea* as I tried to reel in the trout. True, I was no Santiago and this was no marlin, but the struggle was the same.

"It's no use," I panted to Garth, "I can't do it. You pull him in."

In one quick swoop, the fish was out of the water, on the ground, flapping for dear life. I couldn't look. We decided to strike another deal. I'd hook 'em, he'd reel 'em in. Our system worked perfectly, since I was the only one who caught any fish that day.

As days passed, things progressed in much the same way—deal after deal, compromise after compromise. However, toward the end of the week a strange phenomenon occurred. I came to appreciate the solitude, the delicious fresh fish dinners, and the romantic warmth of that cozy stove. I even admitted to Garth that I'd enjoyed our time in the Sierras.

But even though I loved my great outdoorsman, his notions of future wilderness treks with me would have to be relived through memories of snuggles in the A-frame with his little Sacajawea, and photos of our week together.

Because I also had to admit that one adventure was enough for camping wimps like me.

———————◦◇◇◦———————

Marcia Smart considers herself a humorist by nature and has written considerably in this style for many years, earning recognition in the Erma Bombeck international writing contest.

She is also intrigued by psychological anomalies, crime-related drama, and the unexplainable acts people commit against each other. Penning her first foray to the dark side, her book *Constant Killer* (available on Amazon) brings these elements together.

A retired interior redesigner, Marcia has authored DIY books, e-books, and training materials for the design industry.

Marcia lives in Southern California, where she is the organizer for the Conejo Valley Writers group and offers an editing service, www.EditingSmart.net.

THIRTEEN HOURS IN A
DIFFERENT WORLD

J. Schubert

From Camarillo, California, I hopped onto the #50 bus heading to the Oxnard Collection Shopping Mall. It dropped me off and I walked to the Cheesecake Factory. I was early at 11 a.m. I sat outside the restaurant, anticipating my meet-up with friends for lunch. Checked my phone and saw the text: CHEESECAKE FACTORY LUNCHEON CANCELED TODAY.

Now what? What should I do? I'm already here. I walked a few businesses over to Whole Foods. Bought some fresh fruit and a drink, as I hadn't had breakfast. Relaxed inside the dining area and wondered what to do with my day.

Deciding to head to downtown Oxnard, I took the Gold Coast #6 bus. I got off at Hobson Park. A farmers' market was in full swing. A Ranchero band played music. I sat on a park bench listening.

"I've got to grab a meal in a few hours," I mumbled.

Two young men a few feet from me turned in my direction, the taller one saying, "You looking for a meal?

You can get one two blocks away at the Mission, for free. Just show up at 5 p.m."

"What?" I asked.

"The Ventura Mission serves hot meals. You missed lunch, but dinner is at 5 p.m."

"How do you guys know about this?"

"We're homeless, no money, it's the best place to eat. You can even sleep there for the night—if you pass the test."

"Think I'll go check it out, thanks," I said.

Then I thought—the Mission obviously serves a need. I was curious. It would be a good experience as a writer to witness. I made up my mind to go.

Just before 5 p.m., a group of fifty men congregated at the front entrance of the Mission in several unorganized lines. Most were middle-aged, a few in their early twenties. Some disheveled, others appeared to be under the influence of something.

The gates opened to a mad rush inside. A manager with a clipboard pointed to a bench extending along a wall, directing us to have a seat while he took intake. I became a bit uncomfortable now, sitting between these men—some appearing nervous, others fidgeting. Several were excused and asked to leave the premises. I definitely stood out— clean cut, wearing designer jeans, espadrilles, with a leather backpack.

"You're new, haven't seen you here before," said the manager, looking me over.

"Yes, my first time," I responded.

"Well, you blew a zero. Passed the Breathalyzer. Follow me."

He took me into his office. After making a copy of my ID and explaining the process, he told me I needed to take a TB test or I wouldn't be able to return. That I could sleep there for twenty days straight but would have to leave for five before I could return. Finally, he asked me if I would be spending the night. I thought, why not, would be a quick twelve hours. I said "Yes."

Later that evening, I thought about what I would do for five days if I didn't have the sanctuary of the Mission, if I was really homeless.

The meal that evening was baked chicken leg quarters, mixed vegetables, and corn stuffing. It was surprisingly delicious. I asked for seconds after observing others were going back several times. There were various bottled drinks. I settled for water with lemon. This all took place in less than thirty minutes and seemed rushed to me. The only conversation I had was with a man who sat next to me saying, "I made it."

"Made what?"

"I just got off work at the Amazon warehouse a few miles away. It's a struggle to get there on time for dinner. Most of the time they can only save me a spot to sleep," he said.

"Wow, that's a lot to maneuver."

"Just trying to make it work."

About 7 p.m., blankets were distributed. We were all assigned sleeping quarters. The majority of men slept inside in a secured, dorm-style building on bunk beds. Showers were encouraged before bed. There was a dressing room and bathroom. There was no privacy.

I was assigned a cot outside, along with seven other men, in an uncovered patio adjacent to an alley. There was nothing to do after dinner. Our movements were not restricted. Some men got caught up about happenings the past week. I did not speak with any of the other seven. Lighting illuminated the patio, making it difficult to relax and fall asleep. I listened to part of the Dodgers game on my phone before covering my head, nodding off to a broken sleep.

The area was secured and fenced by a five-foot concrete wall. It bothered me how close to the alley we were sleeping. I could hear people walking and talking at all hours of the evening. Several stopped, looking over and into our space. I was awakened once again by a car drag racing in the alley.

I finally woke at 5 a.m. Men were stirring. Realizing it must be time to get up, I went to the bathroom and washed up. After gathering my things, I stood in the breakfast line.

An elderly gentleman, speaking with another man, brought me into their conversation, directing a question to me. As we spoke, I realized this man had a financial background. We exchanged stories about the life of a broker. He told me he was a former Bear Stearns executive. My jaw dropped. Said his girlfriend cleaned out his account, taking off with his whole life savings. That he spent a few years saving his Social Security pension and now was back in the market. His goal was to save enough to cover a year's rent so he could establish housing again. It was hard to imagine that someone with his background could find themselves homeless.

By 6 a.m., we were all fed and directed to exit. I walked over to the park, sat on a bench, thinking how fortunate I've been to have the life I've had.

———————◦◇◆◇◦———————

Andrew Erskine, a.k.a. J. Schubert, grew up in Santa Monica and makes his home in Southern California.

He earned a BA in English and American literature. He writes creative nonfiction and poetry. A recurrent theme in his work centers on the human condition.

MILLIE THE GOLDFISH:
A FABLE ABOUT THE POWER OF BELIEF

Judy Watson

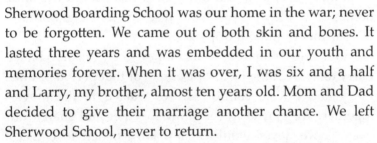

Sherwood Boarding School was our home in the war; never to be forgotten. We came out of both skin and bones. It lasted three years and was embedded in our youth and memories forever. When it was over, I was six and a half and Larry, my brother, almost ten years old. Mom and Dad decided to give their marriage another chance. We left Sherwood School, never to return.

Our grandparents saved our lives and paid for us. Mother had waited and waited for the moment when her life would begin again. It slowly filtered down to her that the only life open to her was with Dad. Her family deserted us, and only Grandma remained. She came to live with us in that year on Winthrop, and Mom could be calm and sane. This was when she began to write fairy tales, which she would read to us in the evening in order to shut out the life that was outside the doors of the apartment.

Years later, I would learn Grandma owned the duplex with her sister Emma. They had bought it for their mother, who lived there until she died. There was no rent and we would be safe on Winthrop.

Father begged to come home. He had no place to go after the war and absolutely no money prospects. He began selling life insurance again, and as his business increased, so did his sexual encounters.

But I was young and full of hope and felt free at last to run—and run I did. Larry, frightened still from the years of horror and anti-Semitism in the boarding school, stayed inside the apartment and drew pictures. If Mom was irrational momentarily and Dad was angry, I could flee for that moment of time.

The two-story building sat across the street from Swift Grammar School. At one time, Swift had served the large homes of wealthy people. Now, it served the neighborhood of apartments and old duplexes.

Somehow Mom found the money to put me into ballet. Larry took art at the Field Museum. For that period of time, Larry and I were comforted. We walked to the movies together. We played in the snow together and shared our lives as we never would again. We listened to classical music on the old Victrola, and I danced and leapt through the air in the front room as Larry sat behind me drawing. We had minimal furniture in that living room, which looked out upon the street below. There was a plain wooden desk, which Larry drew at day in and day out. There was a rocking chair, a small table with a lamp, a radio which became our link to life, and the Victrola which played endless ballets for me to dance to.

The back porch was wooden and so rickety I hoped my endless jumping on it would cause it to collapse, but somehow it withstood me and went on to stand even after we left the next year for California, leaving poverty—or so we hoped—finally behind us.

I have often wondered if that building still exists. It was made of brick, with a perched roof. Everything was crumbling, and the rancid smell of fried onions arose from the ancient, oily, oriental rugs. The apartment was two blocks from Lake Michigan in one direction and two blocks from the "El" in another direction. We lived on the second floor. The screens that enclosed the porch were broken and in need of repair. Safety from the mosquitos that came in the summer heat and the snow that poured in during the winter.

There was no heat that I can recall. In the living room, under the front window, was a radiator, and that was our sole heat in those frigid winters. The winds howled and blew us across the street, and the duplex offered its hand, but the hand was crippled.

The apartment was long and narrow, with a long hallway which had a series of small dark rooms leading off of it. Mother, in a moment of either madness or inspiration, painted the only bathroom fire engine red. The kitchen was in the back of the apartment, and it was here that she began to read her stories to us in the evenings, when the three of us were alone. Dad was never present, and Grandma stayed alone to read in her room.

The entire place smelled of soot, the gray ash from the stockyards settling on every windowsill and in each part of every corner of the duplex. The three of us were like castaways on an inner island that we made for ourselves to push away the ugliness of our surroundings. It was in this period that Mom, always alone, wrote her fairy tales and fables. Her stories were wonderful to us. We were her best and only audience. Each evening, she read to us as the cold winds wrapped themselves around the corners of the old apartment, rattling the glass windowpanes and circulating the damp and cold.

I saw us as three children together. It was just the three of us. Even Grandma was forgotten in those moments when we listened to her stories, which always promised good in the hereafter. The room would fade away, with the only light a bulb dangling on a cord overhead. It became a golden glow for us as we listened in rapture to her stories.

My favorite story was "Millie," a small, forgotten fish who survived as we had and became reborn into a beautiful life. Did this lie ahead for us? Only time would tell.

MILLIE THE GOLDFISH

Once upon a time, in a faraway universe in a wondrous land that never existed, there was an aquarium full of color and light. In that large, special watery existence, where the flow of water caused blue and green lights to flash back and forth, there was a fish called "Millie." How exquisite her many colors were and how special she was swimming in the aquarium among the other fish. Not one other fish had as many beautiful colors of oranges, pinks, blues, and greens. And only Millie had a long, magnificent tail of this rainbow of colors.

As she swam, her tail swept and moved about her as she soared around the aquarium. Her tail was no ordinary tail. Indeed, it was made up of every color imaginable, and its shape and size shone as if a rainbow had bestowed magic upon the fish and its owner. She swam elegantly, haughtily among the other, plainer fish. She was admired, feared, loved, and envied.

Then one day, tragedy struck. Her egotism got the better of her as she was showing off her wondrous tail, and in one dangerous turn and dive she caught her tail in a rock. In one brief moment of time, it broke and shredded. Her magnificent tail of many colors was gone .In shock, Millie, now aware of what her vanity had cost her and understanding she had lost the hallmark of her extraordinary beauty, sank rapidly to the bottom of the aquarium. The other fish quickly ignored and shunned her, as they no longer recognized her. She knew she was different now and that her vanity and foolishness had cost her the one thing in life she loved the most, her exquisite tail. Millie hid in the rocks and gray sand of the aquarium where she had fallen. She remained alone and forgotten.

Days, weeks went by. Millie remained alone and isolated from the other fish. In time, she began to understand and come to terms with her loneliness. Would it always be this way? The sand and rocks buried her from view, and she could not bring herself to look at her reflection again. Gray, black, brown sand was her family now. She watched as the other fish swam back and forth among themselves. She knew that her vanity had cost her everything she had loved.

A period of time went by. The other fish in the aquarium went on with their lives, not noticing Millie anymore. She felt she understood this, and gave great thought to her own vanity and recklessness, which had cost her beauty. She dreamed of another chance, and wondered if it was possible for her to regain her world. If not, indeed, she would be forced to hide forever. Then one day, she accidentally saw her reflection in the glass of the aquarium. At first, she felt she was mistaken. Could it possibly be that her tail had grown back? She slowly swam out of the rocks and glanced back at her tail. To her wonderment, her tail, with all its amazing colors of blue, orange, white, even red, had somehow grown back. She glanced at her reflection and saw that, mystically, she had been restored to her original beauty.

Taking her courage with her, she rose very quietly to the top of the aquarium, through the blue and green reflections of light. The other fish greeted her as if she had never been gone. She understood she had been magically forgiven. Once again, Millie became the queen of her world. Aware she had been given a second chance, Millie vowed to always be kind, loving, and caring to all she met. And best of all, she got to live happily ever after. And as I recall, Millie found her own prince and made little fishes of extraordinary colors who had unique and beautiful tails.

I understand now, as an adult, that "Millie" was more than a story. But the small child sat enthralled and visualized the story of a small, forgotten fish who survived, as we had survived the war. She was reborn into a beautiful life. Did this lie ahead for us? Would the three of us live to fulfill our destinies?

Of course, I do not know the moral of this story, except that in the way of all fables one learns in life, love, loss, grief, and finally finding one's place in the world. Life is an endless glow that beckons us on its path and encourages our bravery to survive.

I can see the three of us yet: the old kitchen, the bare wooden tabletop, the lone light bulb descending over us on its cord, and the evening darkening into night as we listened. Mom's stories told of good in the hereafter, of love and healing. At the end of the year, we left that place. Dad had a chance to go on to a new job, and we moved to California, never to return.

Here was the new beginning. Each of us would take a different path and never forget a small but strong fish whose strength would carry us through.

Judy Watson was born in Chicago, Illinois, and has lived in California since 1947. She is a graduate of Arizona State University, where she majored in literature.

She has two grown children and three grandchildren. Judy currently lives with her two dogs and two cats in Westlake Village, California.

RECOLLECTIONS OF LEE BREUER

Judy Watson

—————————◦◆◇◆◦—————————

Esser Leopold Breuer (Feb. 6, 1937–Jan. 3, 2021) was an American playwright, theater director, academic educator, filmmaker, poet and lyricist. Breuer taught and directed on six continents. (Wikipedia)

Our family came to California in 1947. My father was given a job in a brand-new industry created by the war: women's sportswear. Prior to World War II, women wore dresses. But being forced to take men's jobs, they ended up in pants, and a new world was created and stayed.

We lived in the San Fernando Valley. At that time, before the freeway was built, it was a very lower middle-class neighborhood. It was largely Jewish, and all the kids joined the Jewish Community Center and thrived. Most would go on to UCLA, which in those days was about $67.00 a quarter semester.

The summer I was twelve and a half, my brother allowed me to come along with his friends, newly driving at sixteen, and spend time with them. It was the most memorable and wonderful summer of my childhood. It was then I met Lee Breuer.

He was quiet and beautiful, with his wavy brown hair and big, expressive brown eyes. All the girls had crushes on him. He lived with his mother, a widow, in a small apartment on Moorpark Avenue in Studio City. He did not stand out in any way except for his looks, which drew all the girls.

That summer a little group wrote comedies and performed them at the Jewish Community Center. I do not recall Lee writing anything, but he was always there and part of the group.

All of the boys, including my brother, went to UCLA after they graduated North Hollywood High, as it was affordable for their parents. All went on to be doctors, dentists, lawyers, as was expected of a good Jewish boy. That is, all went on except for my brother, an art major, and Lee. They both joined a Jewish fraternity called Tau Delta Phi. But after a year or two, Lee dropped out. He could not afford the price.

Still, we all kept in touch. I was now seventeen, and it was 1957. My life had gone to hell with my parents' divorce, and I had no place to turn. It was in this period that I got in touch with Lee through my brother. He was living hand to mouth, trying to pay rent and often failing to do so. I recall him telling me how he would jump out of windows to avoid rent collectors. By this time, he was writing plays, and I had no idea about what.

He explained to me that he had drawn the attention of the UCLA admissions by writing a play about a woman who kills her child. She is so poor she throws her child to death so the child will not suffer anymore. UCLA liked this. However, at that time there were no scholarships given by a public institution. They saw his talents but could not help him financially.

One time he had a party at his residence, a reconverted chicken coop, he invited me to a party there. I recall that I had to get down on my hands and knees in order to crawl through the opening of the chicken coop. It was carpeted and without rooms or windows. When I finally got to the back, I was exhausted. Lee was not around, but a young man sat down and introduced himself. He told me he was a professor at UCLA, married, and had just had a child. Then he asked me to have sex with him. I replied, "Didn't you just say you were married and just had a baby?" He looked at me in disgust and said, "You are so bourgeoise," and crept away. I decided I was, so I left and went home.

Lee took me to see *Paths of Glory* (1957), with Kirk Douglas. He was thrilled, and explained to me that my upset and nausea was wonderful and that this movie was truly existential. In other words, hopelessness was the essence of life. I remember that I just nodded my head, which made him happy. He had found a path. I had not.

I saw Lee one last time in 1957, and he was wonderful and kind, and we spent the night like brother and sister. I was being forced to leave California with my mother and stepfather, and that is a story for another day. He knew I was lost. We kissed gently and he promised to write. I think he wrote one letter.

By the time I returned to California, he was gone, and I did not see him for years. I was not surprised. What surprised me was my brother and his friends' great loyalty to Lee and to his desire to write and establish an avant-garde group. At this time, all theatre consisted of three acts, and in the final act we learned, good or bad, what the purpose of the play was. You left the theatre feeling you had learned something that made you feel this was a good ending. Avant-garde theatre here in this country did not exist. Lee was determined to be first and unique, and he was.

That summer, when he was fifteen and I was twelve and a half, we went to his home. I knew when I met his mother, he would leave her as soon as possible. His anger was visible, and you could feel his irritation. She was very much in love with her son. I can still recall her putting her arms around him from behind and seeing him stiffen and move away. I knew he would disappear from her life as fast as possible. It made me sad for her, as it was so obvious she loved him so much, but knew how little she could give him materially.

As the years went by and I had found out from my brother about Lee's marriage and his many "wives" and children, I thought of that day. Nothing would satisfy him, and each time he would know and look ahead to the next woman. He called each one his wife and acknowledged his children as he rushed to the next one. I asked my brother about Ruth (his actual wife) and was told they had "an arrangement."

I did not know my brother and his small circle of friends had continued to give Lee money in order to allow him to live out his dream. Except for my brother, who became well known as a movie illustrator and worked in the arts, the rest had done what their parents wanted and achieved security through various professional jobs.

I saw Lee's photo on a playbill. Where was my beautiful boy? Who was this aging man, bald, with scars? Larry informed me he had a terrible accident. A cappuccino machine had blown up in his face, disfiguring him forever.

Still Larry, who was never wealthy, kept quiet about the money, and then everything changed.

Lee had begun to become famous. Too famous for the boys from Tau Delta Phi. Mabou Mines, an experimental theatre company begun by Ruth and Lee, was becoming known all over the world. I called New York looking for him. It must have been the 1980s. I was now middle-aged, and my son was at UCLA acting. All I could think of was how Lee might help him.

What stands out from that memory is that the office of Mabou Mines ridiculed him to me about money. They were broke. Odd. But they gave me his number, and I called him and found he was coming to California. I invited him, at my expense, to a play at UCLA in which my son, Mitch, was appearing. He agreed to go if I would pick him up, pay for him, and drop him off in Beverly Hills afterward. I agreed.

He watched the play but did not offer to meet Mitch afterwards. Lee insisted we leave so he could get to Beverly Hills and his appointment.

I called my brother soon after. I was terribly unhappy with Lee. It was then Larry told me about all the years of giving and their final great disappointment. "What happened?" I asked. He told me the group went backstage to see Lee after a play that had come to California. They were told Lee was busy and they would have to wait. This was after more than twenty years of financially supporting him. And they were done. I was sorry I had not asked before.

I saw his new wife and hoped she had money. At least he waited for Ruth to die (2013), but was aware she owned half the company of Mabou Mines. I doubt he could afford a divorce.

And then he was dead (2018) and world famous. I don't think he ever missed a beat. And so, I read all the interviews the other day. In one he admits to being Jewish. Well, that was good. I had figured that religion was not part of avant-garde.

In another interview, he blames his poverty on a *New York Times* reviewer who hated him and destroyed every play he mounted. I looked up the reviewer and found he was a German Jew. He preferred theatre as theatre, and despised avant-garde. His reviews were scathing, and quickly shut down plays Lee had mounted or written or directed. What power there was in the old days when all there was was the newspaper.

I read all the interviews and all his comments. I read about the plays, and I really felt like Lee was still in the mindset he had been with me at that movie when we were so young. He had decided then that life was terrible and everything led to an unhappy ending. In Yiddish they say he could "hok a tchynik," meaning he could talk. But his voice was so soft and steady and melodious, you listened. And his steady promotion of his ideas had sold the world, and especially the university world.

Still you have to wonder if therapy would have helped. Instead, he helped himself to a steady diet of women. Was my beautiful boy, always so sad, really a genius? Or was he just angry at his own poverty and lack of power?

And finally, I looked up *The Gospel at Colonus* (1983), his first huge success. The music was written by Bob Telson. Here, in this amazing musical, Lee gained fame permanently. Imagine a musical based on Sophocles and done solely by a black choir.

At that time, Joseph Papp was famous and public theatre in New York was wonderful. This amazing play, which made a star out of Morgan Freeman, also cemented Lee's name in the history of theater. After that, there were many different forms of plays he created. But this one, his first one, was the play of genius. Twenty-six years of struggle, and finally, success. Wealth did not await him. Fame was always just out of reach, and the young boy I had known disappeared into the bald, homely man who now smiled for the camera—but the message remained the same. And though he took advantage of every invitation to teach, direct, write, and visit every country he could, this is the play he will be remembered for.

The lonely, poor Jewish kid with no place to go and no money achieved immortality. Life may be hell but, as Mel Brooks once said, "It is good to be the star."

Mazel tov!

Judy Watson was born in Chicago, Illinois, and has lived in California since 1947. She is a graduate of Arizona State University, where she majored in literature.

She has two grown children and three grandchildren. Judy currently lives with her two dogs and two cats in Westlake Village, California.

THE HISTORY OF THE CONEJO VALLEY WRITERS

The Conejo Valley Writing Group was founded by screenwriter Mike Hayward in December of 2010. What started as a small gathering to find like-minded writers to read and offer critique for his writing and others' soon blossomed into a more formalized "club," complete with elected officers and a strong presence on Meetup.com

Over the years, meetings have been held at coffee shops, homes, and restaurants. Because the CVWriters group meetings have always remained a community outreach endeavor, the Goebel Adult Center in Thousand Oaks, California, graciously opened their doors to the group, where meetings continue to be held monthly.

The group has had several organizers over the years, each offering their time to continue the worthwhile learning experience to help local aspiring writers to develop their skills and hone their manuscripts. Meetings offer a mixture of critique opportunities, writing exercises, and speaker presentations. Located outside Los Angeles presents us with a plethora of professional writers, agents, editors, authors, professors, etc. who graciously offer their expertise, gratis, to enlighten our writers and enrich our meetings. We even had Gene Perrett, Bob Hope's main joke writer for many years. Who says writing isn't fun?

CVWriters are also known for the social aspect we offer in getting to know fellow members in a casual setting. Critique groups have branched off to also include poetry and screenplays, typically meeting independently in person or via social media.

The original mission statement of the group states:

The Conejo-Simi Valley Writers group seeks to bond and strengthen its members in their desire to become better writers, to help them discover how to write at the top of their form, how to edit their work to near-perfection, how to get published...and then to repeat the write-edit-publish formula for the rest of their days.

This group is open to both published and unpublished writers whose interests are expressed across a wide range of formats and genres.

Membership is free.

Thirteen years later, the mission is still being carried forward; albeit tightened to:

"Writers Helping Writers"

ACKNOWLEDGMENTS

Mark Frankcom: So, impressed by the writings of his fellow club members, Mark decided they needed to be collected into an anthology for others to enjoy. He spearheaded the project, starting in January of 2023. If it wasn't for his enthusiasm, this book would not exist.

Thank you, Mark!

Marcia Smart: Coordinator of the Conejo Valley Writers since 2015, she acted as materials organizer and copyeditor for the project. www.EditingSmart.net.

Lynn Varon: A professional copyeditor and member of the Conejo Valley Writers, she helped proofread this project. Her website is www.Varon.com.

Bob Calverley: Co-coordinator and speaker liaison of the Conejo Valley Writers for the past two years, Bob lends his seasoned expertise to provide the perfect "go-to sounding board" for all things writing-related.

Kathryn F. Galán: For excellent formatting and publishing support, www.wynnpixproductions.com.

The Conejo Valley Recreation and Parks District, and the Goebel Center staff and administration for their assistance and generosity in giving us a room (since 2010) to hold our monthly meetings, thus helping our writers group find a true "home."

Made in the USA
Monee, IL
08 January 2024

50414408R00111